A FAMILY LIKENESS

By the same author

A FAMILY
LIKENESS

and other stories
by Mary Lavin

CONSTABLE
LONDON

First published in Great Britain 1985
by Constable and Company Limited
10 Orange Street London WC2H 7EG
Copyright © 1985 by Mary Lavin
Set in Monophoto Garamond 12 pt by
Servis Filmsetting Ltd, Manchester
Printed in Great Britain by
St Edmundsbury Press
Bury St Edmunds, Suffolk

British Library CIP data
Lavin, Mary
A family likeness
I. Title
823'.912[F]   PR6023.A91/

ISBN 0 09 466670 9

Contents

A Family Likeness

'Laura, it's nearly April. There might be primroses in the woods,' Ada threw out this idle comment while she and her daughter sat over mid-morning coffee, waiting until it was time to lift Daff. Daff was four, but she woke at cockcrow, and most mornings had to be put down again for a nap.

'What a good idea, Mother. Let's go over the minute she wakes.' Laura sprang up and went to the window to look across the fields towards the small beech wood on the rim of the property. Clearly she was picturing clumps of primroses dotting the brown loam under the trees, each one set like a posy made by hand in a collar of green leaves. 'I wonder if I ought to wake her? She's down long enough.' Laura was making for the hall. 'Daff?' she called softly up the stairs. Then she called a little louder. 'Daff?'

Ada was torn between a conviction that no child can ever get too much sleep and a hankering for her little granddaughter's chatter, Ada wished that Laura and Richard would give up that silly pet name. The name Daphne was so nice. 'It's a wonder you don't call her Dotty,' she said irritably when Laura came back to the table.

'Oh, drop it, Mother, please,' Laura said. They'd been over this ground once too often. But she didn't mean to offend. 'Whose baby is she anyway?' she added. This was a standing joke between them ever since Daff was born and had several times served to head off one of the sudden squalls that no amount of tact, no amount of love could stop from blowing up out of a clear sky.

Ada, who suspected she was being let down lightly, made a timid attempt to have the last word. 'It's not fair to such a pretty child,' she said.

'She is sweet, isn't she?' Laura said, to put an end to the argument, and when next moment there was a footfall on the upper landing both women rushed to the foot of the stairs, Ada to throw out her arms for Daff to jump into them, Laura to gather up an armful of wraps from the bannister rail. For all the sunshine, there could be a nip in the air. 'Let's not waste a minute,' Laura urged, poking Daff's arms into the sleeves of a fleecy white coat Ada had bought her.

Ada closed her eyes. A child's arms were so fragile and when Laura turned and attempted to force her, too, into a coat, she pulled away. 'This coat is yours, Laura.'

'What matter?' Laura was so off-hand, Ada hesitated to protest further.

When Laura was growing up and quite plump, and she herself was still in full sail, Laura never disclaimed borrowing one of her dresses and blouses. Now it was Ada who was glad to avail herself of an occasional cast-off, a raincoat or dressing gown, or even laddered stockings if the run was in the heel or thigh where it didn't really show. But this coat was so roomy, Ada sighed. Age had pared her to the bone like a field made spare by wintry winds. 'I could easily run up and get my own coat, Laura.'

'Why bother?'

Why indeed? With another sigh, Ada folded the coat around her, and the trio, all muffled up, set out for the woods. There was indeed a nasty nip in the air, but only in the shade of the house. When they got beyond the shadow of the gable it was really warm for the time of year. To get to the woods, they had to climb over a stile.

'Here, let grandmother help you, Daff,' Ada offered.

'Oh, leave her alone, Mother. She's well able to manage.'

Better than me, Ada thought ruefully when she had to be helped over the stile, not Daff. Daff was already manfully plunging through grass up to her middle. The growth was truly remarkable for April. It promised well for their finding at least a few primroses.

Laura was in great form. 'Let's make Daff a tossy-ball, Mother, like you used to make me when I was small. I never did figure out how you got the flowerheads all bunched up together without the stems showing.'

'Black thread. I used to bring a spool of it in my pocket. I wish we had thought of bringing one with us today.' Ada was not really attending to what Laura was saying. She was watching Daff progress. The long grass was heavy going for a four-year-old. Then her attention returned to her daughter. 'Tossy-balls are made with cowslips, not primroses, Laura.'

'Oh, well. Maybe we'll find cowslip too.'

'Not in the woods. They're only found in pasture, or meadow.' Ada looked around. 'There might even be some in this field.' She gave a violent start. 'Do I see cattle?' Instinctively, she grabbed Daff by the hand.

'Take it easy, Mother. The cattle are over at the far end. They only come back here to shelter for the night. Grass near trees is too sour for them. See. They're lying down. No wonder. It's a glorious day.'

Ada stifled her fears as best she could by watching Daff plodding valiantly onwards. To Ada herself, the wood was proving farther away than she'd bargained on. 'Ought we carry her, do you think, Laura?'

'You? Or me?' Laura's voice was scalding. 'You don't

seem to realize it, Mother, but she's a big lump now. Sometimes you really astonish me. You know I'm not supposed to over-exert myself these days.' She gave Daff a poke in the back. 'Hurry up,' she said. But sensing Ada's disapproval, her next remark was transparently an attempt to please. 'This was a really good idea of yours, Mother.'

'I hope you won't be disappointed,' Ada said, non-commitally. Her glance roved over to a grassy bank. In all truth, she was having misgivings herself about their outing. 'Now I come to think of it, a wood is not really the right place to find primroses either. Primroses grow best on a sunny bank.' She pointed, 'Like over there. Look. What did I tell you?' Indistinct, but ummistakable as the glow of stars in the Milky Way, masses and masses of primroses studded the green bank.

'Oh. Do you not want to go any farther, Mother? Is that it?' Laura asked. 'You could go back from here, if you wish, and I could take Daff to the edge of the woods and let her get a glimpse of ...'

'Of what? The primroses are on the bank.'

'That's right.' Laura ceded graciously enough. 'Well, suppose you and Daff go over there and you sit down, while she picks a little bunch, and I go on to the woods. It's ages since I've been over there and it's important I keep fit.'

Fine as the prick of the smallest needle ever made, one with an eye so narrow it was quite impossible to thread, Ada's heart was pierced with sadness. Had her daughter seen that she was failing? She, who up to such a short time ago had been indefatigable, possessed indeed of far more energy than Laura herself had ever enjoyed.

'I don't want to sit down, Laura,' she said. With a pang she remembered the way her own mother had laid a querulous emphasis on some words. 'The grass may be damp,' she added meekly.

'Damp? That bank, with the sun pouring down on it since dawn?' Laura laughed, but glancing at her mother, she seemed to suffer a change of heart. 'I suppose it wouldn't be any harm for us all to take a short rest,' she said. 'Come on, Daff. This way.'

Why did she have to speak so peremptorily to the child, Ada wondered. 'The primroses are over there, dear,' she explained. When Daff didn't budge, she appealed to Laura. 'The child really is tired,' she said.

'All to the good. Maybe after this she might sleep through the night for a change.' Laura swung around savagely. 'Last night, she woke me at least three times.'

'I didn't hear a sound. Why didn't you call me?' Ada tried to keep her voice down.

'And if I did?'

Ada was not sure if her daughter meant she could be of no use or if she was insinuating that she might not have been prepared to get up and help. She looked dejectedly into the grass. 'Why didn't you call me?' 'Why?' she persisted.

Laura turned a cold eye on her. 'Haven't I heard you say often enough that there is no sweeter music than the crying of another woman's child.'

Oh, oh, oh! How Laura could twist words. Ada was outraged. 'Not your child, Laura. Not my own grandchild. Not Daff.' She could not remember having said such a thing unless perhaps to put some young mother at ease in a hotel if an infant had been wailing in the night. 'I do wish you had called me, Laura.'

'Don't go on and on about it. Please. It's not as if it was only last night. Every night is the same. I'm worn to a frazzle. I scarcely ever close an eye.'

They had started to walk on, when, nearing the headland, under their feet where the grass was scant, Ada saw a cow-pat. 'I thought you said the cattle didn't graze here,' she said, and hurrying, she made for the bank. From it she scanned the field. 'I can't see them anymore. Where have they gone?' she asked anxiously. There was more than one cow-pat. She saw several.

'Who cares?' Laura turned aside. 'Well, Daff? What do you think of the primroses?' The primroses were unbelievably plentiful. 'Can I pick them?' Daff asked in awe.

'Of course, darling.'

'This is how we do it, Daff.' Ada forgot the cattle. Burrowing, with fingers still nimble, down between the thick leaves of a large clump that bore twenty flowers or more, she grubbed close to the roots and pinched off a primrose with a long stem, cool and green, its base softly flushed with pink. 'We don't want to pull off their poor heads, do we?' she said gaily. 'And we'll only take one from each clump, so there'll be some left for other people to enjoy.' It was such a pleasure to guide the young mind. She was glad to see that Daff was watching intently. There ought to be no need of a scolding next time she beheaded a flower in the garden.

'For goodness' sake, Mother. They're only wild flowers. Let her enjoy them.'

'She could hardly be enjoying them more,' Ada said as Daff proudly held up a primrose with a stem as long as a beanstalk. 'It's precisely because these are wild that we can teach her how to pick flowers properly.' She guided Daff's hand into the moist depths of another clump. Then, seeing that Daff had got the hang of things, she began to pick a bunch herself to bring back to her room, taking care to pick a few leaves to make a collarette for them. But when Laura, disregarding the fact that she was crushing several clumps, lowered herself down on the bank and lay back to bask in the sun, she was instinctively impelled to caution her. 'It's too early in the season for that, Laura.'

Laura sat up at once, but only the better to deliver an angry retort. 'I don't care if I get pneumonia. You haven't the faintest notion how exhausted I am, Mother. When I was Daff's age, you had servants to wait on you hand and foot.'

Taken off her feet by this outburst, Ada abruptly sat down. 'You are greatly mistaken, Laura. The only help I ever had was an incompetent local girl who came in for a few hours to do a bit of cleaning. I never let her into the nursery.'

'More fool you.' Laura let her head flop back on the grass.

Ada stared. What had precipitated this attack? 'Your father, of course, was wonderful,' she said. 'If you woke at night it was him, not me, who walked the floor with you.'

Again, Laura sat bolt upright. 'Are you insinuating that Richard does not pull his weight? You forget he provides for us. The child is my concern.'

'No one is disputing that. Don't think, dear, I haven't noticed how tired you've been looking lately. It's not easy for me to see you so white and drawn.'

Laura, who lay with her beautiful face framed in flowers, made a move as if to sit up for the third time, but instead she turned her head and fixed on Ada a stare that went through her, not like a needle this time, but a pitchfork.

'Just exactly what are you trying to do to me, Mother? Bad enough to feel like hell without being told I look like hell.'

'Did I say that?' Ada stared miserably at the bunch of wild flowers in her hand. 'Here, Daff, you can have mine,'

she said. Daff shook her head, her interest in primroses was
waning. The few she'd picked were scattered about on the
grass. Ada left her own bunch down beside them, where it
fell apart, the stems now looking more pink than green.
Like worms, she thought, shuddering. She ought perhaps
to dredge up from the time of her own young motherhood
some experience or other that would show Laura she
understood her fatigue. She hit on one at once. 'My own
mother used to drive me mad when you were small, telling
me I'd some day look back on those years as the best years
of my life.' But hearing herself repeat the timeworn words,
Ada felt that the old adage was true. Then suddenly Laura
launched into a gratuitous and glowing reminiscence of her
grandmother, a reminiscence which, in the circumstances,
could only be intended to hurt.

'Poor Grandmother. I used to feel so sad when you were
mean to her.'

'Mean? Me?' Ada winced.

Laura, who surely could see the wound she'd inflicted,
was in no way repentant. 'I loved her. She was such a dear
little thing, so gay and happy most of the time. She was
always overwhelmed with gratitude when I went up to her
room and listened to her stories. She had an unending store
of them. We had such fun. We used to laugh so much the
two of us when we were together.'

'At what?' Ada was disconcerted. And when Laura
smiled enigmatically she was goaded into self-justification.
'Towards the end of her life your grandmother made
things very difficult for me. I can tell you that.'

'You didn't understand her. That was your problem,'
Laura said so smugly that Ada looked away in disdain. The
sun still spilled down but she felt chill as if it had gone
behind a cloud. 'She used to brush my hair,' Laura added
and closed her eyes.

To Ada there was something bogus about her daughter's nostalgia. 'When it suited her,' she snapped. 'Any time I needed her help she always seemed to have something more important of her own to do.'

'Like what?' Laura opened one eye.

'This and that.' Ada was flustered at being pinned down. 'Well, for one thing, she was forever reading newspapers, even papers a week old.'

'What else?'

'Let me see. She spent hours and hours cutting out snippets of news that apparently had some special significance for her. God knows why. The same with magazines. Oh yes, another thing, she had a collection of old postcards that she was always sorting.' Ada paused. Somehow these occupations of her mother's didn't seem sufficient to account for the awful clutter in that little room of hers. 'She used to hoard string and spend hours taking out the knots or tying together bits too small to be of any use. Your father often asked me to try and get her to keep her door shut. Of course, she never did. Your grandmother was a law unto herself.'

'I don't see that it mattered whether her door was open or shut, way up there at the top of the house. No one ever went up there, only him and me and whoever brought up her meals.'

'It was *me* who brought them up. Who else did you think? I always had to bring trays up to her because she never came down at proper meal-times. She was really wilful about small things. And if she did condescend to come down, it would be in her own good time, when the washing-up was done, the pots and pans put away, and the kitchen swept. You know how annoying that can be to a servant.'

'No.' As if the monosyllable was not sufficiently deadly,

Laura went on. 'Old people can't be expected to be exactly normal.'

'She was the same as far back as I can remember,' Ada protested. 'I cannot recall her ever doing anything at the right time. When I was young, my meal was never on the table when I came home from school. She didn't even have the supper ready in the evening when my father came home tired and hungry from the office. She thought nothing of keeping us waiting while she attended to some fiddle-faddle.'

'Such as?'

'Oh.' Ada sighed wearily. Those memories of her mother were becoming too painful to contemplate. 'In those days, I think it was letter-writing,' she said apathetically. 'She'd sit for hours at the dining-room table dashing off page after page and then she'd go out to the pillar box before she'd pay any attention to us.'

'Letters to whom?'

'How do I know?' Ada was exasperated by this inquisition, but just then it was as if a shaft of light fell on the hand of that long-dead letter writer and she was confounded by what it revealed. 'Wait, Laura. I *do* know. She was writing to her own mother. To my grandmother. How could I have forgotten?' She wrote to her every other day, long interminable letters.'

'I'm not surprised. She dearly loved her own mother. She was always talking about her,' Laura said dreamily. Then unexpectedly she opened both eyes and a look of amazement came on her face. 'Good Lord. Your mother's mother would be Daff's great- great-grandmother. You don't mean to say you remember her, Mother?'

'Why, yes of course I remember her. My mother kept a photograph of her beside her bed. I remember she had large dark eyes, soft and liquidy with a curiously vulnerable look, like a doe or a gazelle. I assure you too that my mother's constant talk about her made her a real presence in our house.' Again, Ada had a vision of the dead hand, barely able to constrain the love that sent its pen racing over the paper. 'I suppose I was jealous of my grandmother,' she said reflectively. 'I resented her place in my mother's affections, not only for myself but for my father too. I hated her. Although looking back now I realize she had a hard life. After all, she had twelve children. Can you imagine that? I suppose it was no wonder my own mother was so devoted to her, I may have been unfair as well as unforgiving.'

Laura surprisingly put out her hand and patted her knee. 'It's all so long ago, how can one say?' she said. 'And does it really make any difference now?'

Ada appreciated the gesture, even if the words were tactless. 'I'm sometimes sorry that I didn't listen more to her when she was talking about the past. I never seemed to have the time.'

'One can always make time,' Laura's mood had changed again. 'As I remember it, you expected her to be always at your beck and call just because she was living with you.'

Ada found this so unforgiveable, she had to change the subject quickly. 'What is Daff doing?' she asked, although the child was only a few yards away and appeared perfectly happy. But as she spoke, Daff gave a rapturous squeal and she saw that, bored by the primroses, she had wandered back to the cow-pat and was about to poke her fingers in it. 'Laura. Stop her,' Ada yelled. She herself could never have got to her feet in time.

Laura stood up clumsily. 'Daff. Don't touch that, you little fool,' she yelled, catching the child and shaking her.

'Do you want to get filthy? Come away from there, at once.' Dragging Daff after her she came back to the bank, out of breath.

'It was probably dried up,' Ada said, hoping to make light of things.

'If she stuck her fingers in it, we'd soon know whether it was dry or not.' Ada was chastened. Laura did look tired; she had eased herself down on the bank once more and closed her eyes again leaving Daff standing uncertainly in front of her.

Ada felt the child had done enough penance. 'You can play anywhere you like, dear, as long as you don't get yourself dirty,' she said. But Daff still stood unhappily waiting for her mother to speak to her. After a minute, Ada had to resort to the well-known bait for catching a parent's attention. 'Who is Daff like, do you think, Laura?' she asked.

Laura did not rise to the bait. 'Who cares?' she said.

'That depends.'

'What do you mean by that?' Laura warily opened one eye.

'Well, you can be thankful that you resemble your grandmother, my dear,' Ada said. To her dismay, she saw Laura's expression change instantly from suspicion to vexation. 'I know dear that when I said this before it upset you, but ...'

'Is it any wonder? When I was small you were always threatening that I'd grow up to be like her.'

'Oh, I meant that I wouldn't have wished you to inherit her character. But in her prime, my mother was a very beautiful woman, and one couldn't wish better for you than that you'd take after her in looks. Say what you like, you do. You are the living image of her.

'You used to be upset, dear, because you knew her only when she was an old woman. When she was young her face was like the face on a Greek coin. And to the last her skin was smooth and soft. It was that olive texture which never shows wrinkles, unlike mine, or for that matter, yours. Don't misunderstand me. I've always been proud of your porcelain skin, but that type of skin is never as durable as an olive complexion.' Here, she bent over and scrutinized her daughter's face. 'Laura. Are you listening? I hope you put some protection on your face, specially when you go out in the harsh wind. If you don't, you'll wake up one day with broken veins. But to go back to the resemblance between you and my mother. Do you know that photograph of her wearing a white blouse in broderie anglaise, with her lovely chestnut hair piled on the top of her head, the one where she's holding me in her arms? She was very young when that was taken.' Suddenly, Ada gasped. 'Why, Laura. she must have been only your age then. Let me see.' She began to make a quick count on her fingers. 'I simply can't believe it. You are already older now than she was then. A year older at least. No, two years. Laura, are you listening to me at all?' she asked. She leant over her again. Laura was asleep.

Ada felt as desolate as if Laura had gone away and left her alone. Then she remembered Daff. Daff was poking at something with that twig. The cow-pat? No. But yes. The child was stirring it up and now she had released upon the air an utterly disgusting smell. Ecstatically then, the child began to flick at it, sending the soft wet dung raining down on her dress, her face and her shining hair.

'Laura. Laura.' Ada shook her daughter. 'Quick. Wake up. Daff's at the dung again.' Her own exhaustion was so great she could not attempt to cope.

A Walk on the Cliff

Ordinarily, Maud drove like a fury. Today, too, she flung her luggage into the boot of her car and was on the road to Waterford well before the hour suggested by her son-in-law. Longing to see her daughter again she wanted to arrive in time to see everything – specially the view from the house.

Speeding through the Midlands she was indifferent to the beauty of the fields lit by the rich, yellow sunlight of the early autumn day.

Maud had not seen her daughter since the day she watched the happy pair drive off after the wedding reception, a troupe of slightly tipsy young people running down the driveway behind the car, bombarding it with confetti. In the intervening months her heart had ached with a loneliness no letters, no phone calls, could assuage.

Since she was a child Veronica had tried to take her dead father's place in their lives, valiantly striving to cope with Maud's many self-acknowledged failings. Better still, the girl had always made light of the failings – cigarettes stubbed out in tea cups, pencil parings blocking the hand basin – that sort of thing.

How Maud missed her. Not just for her help and companionship but for a unique quality of wit and sensitivity she had never found in anyone else. She was not fool enough to think that her loneliness would be cured by

this one overnight visit, but it was her own wish to stay
only a single night. Veronica, and Denis too, had pressed
her to stay longer, for a weekend at least, but she had been
adamant. Still, she did not want to miss a minute of it, the
visit being long overdue.

The newly-weds had got it hard to find a house in the
city. They had been forced to stay in a hotel for the first six
weeks of their marriage, and when they finally hit on a
house it was eight miles outside the city, in a small fishing
port popular in summer as a family resort. Maud had easily
guessed what that meant – young parents with lots of
children whose main requirement of a villa would be a low
rent and plenty of beds. The same families had probably
been going there summer after summer for years on end
and few would defect until their children would be old
enough to be taken abroad. And when a family did drop
out, the owner of the villa would no doubt have a long
waiting list of other well recommended families suitable in
need and kind. Veronica had recognized, and written to
acquaint her mother, that the people who owned the villas
were chary of anyone like herself and Denis looking for
rental on a year-round basis. Accommodation was harder
to get in winter than in summer, because in the off-season
the owners, mostly widows or widowers, retired persons at
any rate, on a fixed income, depended for some semblance
of home life on claiming back their delapidated properties.
No doubt they spent the dreary wintry months attempting
to stave off the total collapse of their villas, foraging in junk
shops for spare parts of electric appliances no longer on the
market, or conning over contracts and inventories in hopes
of getting compensation for sofas and soft furnishings
damaged not by tenants but by time.

Veronica and Denis seemed to have been remarkably

lucky in finding a villa whose elderly owner had to go to Jamaica for an indefinite period to care for a brother unexpectedly invalided. According to one of Veronica's letters the sole merit of the villa was its availability, although Maud felt that must be open to question since it was at the seaside. Surely that counted for something?

All her life Maud had yearned to live by the sea but she had invested so much of herself in her home in County Meath and her beautiful garden, she could never seriously contemplate moving. Yet oh how she loved the sea! And when a signpost showed that she was nearing the coast, she slowed down to catch the first glimpse of the ocean. To her amazement, it had been in sight for some time. She had taken sea to be sky, and mistook for flecks of mist, far-out waves capped by an off-shore wind. Stopping the car at once, she got out to fill her lungs with the salty air, half-hoping her ear might catch the boom of surf. Not near enough yet for that enchanting sound, she continued on her way.

There was a mist rising. The day was changing. Arriving at last in the little port, which was still smaller than she had expected, she found it lay between two headlands and a real fog had collected in the hollow. She changed down into first gear and drove slowly along the main street on which the entire community of villas seemed to be congregated, all much of a muchness, weatherbeaten and depressing. Any number of these shabby villas had ramshackle verandas. For that matter any number of them could have been called yellow. And all the gardens were the same, a straggle of unruly fuchsia bushes, a dismal array of puce petunias, claimed by seedsmen to thrive near the sea, by which they meant that in the salty air they were among the few flowers that would survive there. To make matters more confusing for her, in front of every hall door there was the same apron of ill-assorted pebbles and crushed sea-shells, obviously barrowed up by hand from such stretch of fore-shore as one must surmise to exist here somewhere if the place really was a place for children to have any fun.

Not finding the house, she was forced to turn the car on a cement ramp that must run down to a harbour, because she could see the top of a lighthouse over a shambles of sheds and warehouses.

Voyaging back along the street for the second time, quite forgetting she had arrived earlier than expected, Maud felt piqued that Veronica was not on the look-out for her, or had at least been more explicit with directions, when, to her joy she heard her daughter's voice.

'Mother! We didn't expect you so soon. How did you make it so fast? You must have driven like a demon.' Appearing out of the least likely of the villas, Veronica was strugglng to wrench open its corroded iron entrance gates.

Understanding that she was intended to bring her car inside Maud sat waiting until with a shrug Veronica gave up on the gates and ran out through a side-gate that was wide open, permanently so, Maud judged, since it was off one of its hinges and fast embedded in the ground. 'Let's leave the car on the street.' Veronica said airily. 'Denis can bring it in later.' She leant forward and gave Maud a kiss, which was disconcerting. They never used to bother kissing. 'What time did you leave home?' she asked. 'I'm afraid you really do drive dangerously. I worry about you.' She took Maud's arm in a way Maud found offensively solicitous.

'Stop fussing!' Irritated by a new, matronly tone in her daughter's voice, Maud disengaged her arm, ostensibly to lock the car.

'There's no need to lock it, Mother,' Veronica said. 'We

never lock ours. Come inside and we'll have a drink. Unless you'd prefer tea.'

'Oh tea is a nuisance,' Maud shook her head. A cup of tea would be very nice but she knew Veronica would feel obliged to provide all the paraphernalia of saucers, spoons, a cream jug, a sugar basin and God knows what else. Anyway, just then Denis appeared, and from Veronica's shriek of surprise Maud guessed he must have come home early in compliment to his mother-in-law. She could not but be pleased. His greeting was as cordial as anyone could possibly wish, and she liked the masterful way he put out his hand for the keys of the car, yanked open the rusty gate and drove her car up to the hall door. But when he opened the luggage compartment, and she saw his look of stupefaction at all the puck she'd brought, she would have been abashed if Veronica had not giggled.

'Don't be alarmed, Denis,' Veronica said. 'Mother always brings as much stuff with her for a night as for a week.'

Maud felt exonerated by the giggle. She had never seen the sense of trying to pack properly when travelling by car. She just stuffed jumpers, shoes and odds and ends of underclothes into one case. Things likely to crush she put into another and roomier case. Coats, mackintoshes and wellington boots she simply put on the back seat. And surely it was only commonsense to segregate jars, bottles of stuff that might spill, in a separate case by themselves.

She caught Denis by the sleeve. 'There's no need to bring in everything,' she said. 'Just that one.' She pointed at random to one of the cases, trying hard to remember what was in it. 'And perhaps that small one,' she added apologetically, thinking her sleeping pills might be in that one.

Denis however was proceeding to methodically unload everything.

Resigned Maud looked on until he was about to lift out a fourth case, an old one, at the back.

'Not that one,' she said, putting out a hand to stop him. 'That one is empty.' As she saw her son-in-law stare at her in utter incomprehension she turned and appealed to her daughter. 'Veronica, you know how an empty spare case can come in handy sometimes, in case you see something you want to buy or –' She broke off impatiently. 'You were often glad enough to avail yourself of my oddity in this respect. Do you remember –'

But Veronica was not listening. She too was peering into the boot.

'What on earth have you got in all those cardboard boxes, Mother?'

'What ones? Oh those!' Maud had forgotten them. 'Those are the wedding presents you left behind, the ones you said could wait till someone was coming down here. And so –'

'How very thoughtful of you,' Denis said, politely, and then very pleasurably he repeated his thanks as he pulled into view the gift-wrapped boxes which Maud had tied up again with their silver strings and ribbons. 'Thank your Mother, Veronica,' he prompted, rather patronizingly Maud thought. Not that she wasn't secretly pleased because as far as Veronica was concerned she might have spared her pains. Her daughter was still poking about in the boot. When she spoke it was without turning around.

'There's no need for thanks. We could have collected them ourselves sometime. And we know what's in them. I've already written and thanked for them. I had thought of trying to change those things if the dockets were with

them. I hope you kept them if they were enclosed?'
Without waiting for an answer she ducked her head back
into the boot. 'Ah here is something that does not belong
to us. The seal is not even broken on it.' Dragging at it, she
revealed a heavy carton, but she had the grace to blush
when she saw the carton bore the label of a well-known
wine merchant. 'Oh Mother, you shouldn't have done
that,' she said, realizing it was for them. When Maud saw
Denis grin at his wife's discomfort she warmed towards
him, yet when having deposited her goods and chattels on
the veranda he came back and prepared to usher her
towards the house, she pulled back.

'Aren't you going to lock the car?' she asked.

'But it's inside our gate.'

'All the same! Your wedding presents are in it,' she said,
in open dismay. With difficulty she forebore to mention the
wine was in it too.

'We can take them in later if it worries you,' Denis said.
Exasperated Maud decided to avoid further argument
by whisking the car keys out of his hand. 'If you don't
mind!' she said impatiently, locking not only the boot and
the driver's door, but trying the other doors as well. Then
she allowed him to take her elbow, and be led inside.

In the hall Veronica, brisk as a porter, made straight for
the stairs. 'I'll show Mother her room, Denis,' she called
back.

'Wouldn't she like a drink first?' Denis called up the
stairs after them, because Veronica was already half-way up
and Maud had felt she had no option but to follow.
Looking down between the bannisters she noted with
approval a generous array of drinks laid out on a big
Victorian sideboard.

Upstairs Veronica opened the door of a large airy front

bedroom, its walls newly and tastefuly papered. Except for the bed, though, the room was practically empty.

'What a lovely room,' Maud exclaimed truthfully enough, because the large uncurtained windows showed up, emphasized, the room's fine proportions, as well as its bareness.

Denis meanwhile, who had bumped his way up the narrow stairs with the cases, joined in the chat. 'It is a nice room, isn't it? You should have seen it when we first took possession of the place. It was full of junk but we lugged it all up to the attic and stowed it away out of sight.'

For a dreadful moment it crossed Maud's mind that this might be their own room vacated for her visit, until she noticed that the bed was an exceedingly small single bed.

'Will you be alright here, Mother? Comfortable?' Veronica asked, obviously as proud as her husband of the freshness and brightness of the room. 'Is there anything you might need, Mother?' she asked quite innocently.

To have answered in the negative would seem so sarcastic Maud thought it tactful to make a small request. 'Perhaps I could have a second pillow?' she asked. She sometimes read in bed for a few minutes, although she always jettisoned her second pillow before putting out the light and settling down to sleep.

It was really flattering to see how Denis dashed off to grant this simple behest. A regular cavalier! Maud thanked him profusely when he came back with the pillow. Then she thought no more of it. And when he said he'd go down and fix the drinks she wondered if he was not perhaps being tactful and leaving Veronica and herself alone. She smiled happily at her daughter. 'Well?' she said.

Veronica had gone over to the window. 'Come and look out, Mother. You can get a glimpse of the sea from this room.'

'It's at *you* I want to look my darling,' Maud said, and turning down the bedspread she kicked off her shoes and flopped down on the bed. 'Sit down and tell me all your news.'

Veronica looked back over her shoulder. 'What about the dinner?'

'Oh bother the dinner. It's early yet. Just a little minute. I've been so lonely for you. How *are* you, darling?'

This time Veronica swung round. 'I'm fine. Why did you ask?'

Why indeed? Maud couldn't see that the question was anything but natural, although she was certainly made uncomfortable at having asked it. 'You look marvellous, absolutely marvellous. Only it's so long since I saw you I wondered how things were going with you.'

'What on earth do you mean by that?' Veronica demanded.

Oh dear. Maud stood up. 'Can I give you a hand with the dinner?' she asked.

Veronica seemed to relax. 'Not really,' she said, somewhat shamefacedly. 'As a matter of fact I have everything prepared. I've only to turn on the oven. Actually we thought we'd take you for a walk if you came before dark. And since you have come so early we ought to take advantage of it and show you the sights. First, let's have that drink though.'

Judging by the speed with which she was shepherded down the stairs, Maud gathered that the drink would be a quick one. And in the living room, which they had made extraordinarily attractive with books and prints and lots of pot plants, there was a log fire blazing boisterously. How good it would be to sink into one of the big shapeless armchairs in front of that fire, Maud thought. Denis did proffer a chair of course, but she declined it. If she sat down she'd never be persuaded to get up again.

They had their drinks standing, and in no time at all they were out in the street again.

'Well? Where will we take her?' Denis asked Veronica. The young people went into consultation and while they did Maud looked around in mild wonder at there being much of a choice.

'How about the pier?' Denis said.

'I thought perhaps a walk on the cliff,' Veronica said.

'It's too misty for the cliff, dear,' Denis said, and in spite of the endearment he spoke authoritatively.

'So love, to the pier,' Veronica agreed, giving in so easily Maud stared at her. She was always gentle but she had had a mind of her own for all that.

They set off.

At the ramp where Maud had turned her car Denis paused. 'This is the new fish factory,' he said, proudly pointing to a particularly ugly concrete structure before leading them onward once more. 'I'm afraid there won't be many trawlers in the port at this hour,' he said. 'It's too early.' Maud wondered if he could be censorious about her early arrival, but put it out of her head. There had been no need for him to come home early if he hadn't wanted to do so. He was probably thinking entirely of her getting the maximum enjoyment out of their excursion.

On the quay, which was stacked with wooden crates, and criss-crossed with a regular cat's cradle of ropes and steel hawsers which made it difficult to walk, there was nevertheless a lot of fuss and bustle. There were only two trawlers, but the catch had evidently been exceptional and everyone was discussing it. Yapping dogs abounded. And as another trawler rounded the lighthouse a cheer went up. Its hold glistened with fish, even in the gathering mist.

'It's exciting here, isn't it, Mother?' Veronica squeezed her arm enthusiastically.

Maud let her own reaction be assumed the same. She could not really say in so many words that she enjoyed the sight of the heaving mass of fish in the belly of the trawler nearest them. 'Why are they moving?' she whispered anxiously. Luckily Veronica did not hear because Maud had realized the fish were dead. They only slithered about when the trawler rocked in the back-wash of a wave slapping against the quayside.

'You can see into the cabins through the lower portholes if you bend down, but you've got to be discreet,' Veronica rattled on while Maud tried to listen without looking at what she was being shown. 'Mother, you should see the place at night when the lights are on. You can stare into the cabins all you like then because the men have gone off to the pubs.' The girl was in really good fettle now. 'One night a few weeks ago a Dutch trawler was caught inside the twelve-mile limit, and the maritime police went out and arrested it. They brought it back into the harbour here under escort. The whole catch was confiscated. Can you imagine the scene, the swearing and cursing? It was a wet night but Denis and I got up and came down to see the spectacle. Everyone in the place came down.'

'I'm sure it was fun,' Maud said so tepidly she felt obliged to make an effort to display a less remote interest. 'Do you ever get any fish free?' she asked.

'We never ask for it, if that's what you mean,' Veronica said. Her voice was cold again. 'The whole catch is salted and boxed and sent straight off to the city market. An odd time a local fisherman throws us out a few mackerel. But we'd never dream of asking.'

'Sorry!' Maud said, almost in self mockery, her transgression seemed so slight. Veronica's sanctimony galled her. She was delighted, however, to see it was not lost on Denis either, although she knew he would have to be tactful with his wife.

'Mackerel is not a very popular fish,' he explained to Maud. 'It's regarded as a scavenger. Fresh out of the sea though and properly cooked, the way Veronica does it, can be delicious. We have developed a real passion for it.'

Devoutly Maud prayed they were not intending to indulge that particular passion at dinner tonight. And unfortunately just then her eye fell on a number of lobster baskets piled on the foredeck of one of the trawlers.

'Do you ever get a lobster?' she found herself asking impulsively. When the others exchanged a glance she could not read, she saw how she'd blundered. 'How stupid of me,' she hurried to add. 'Lobsters are almost unobtainable these days, aren't they? I suppose if they do get any – ' her glance stole back in spite of herself to the lobster pots ' – they're despatched at once to London or Paris. I know that in New York they are priced out of sight, except those huge Caribbean ones that are so tough and tasteless. Caviare is easier to get – and cheaper.' Oh dear! Now they would think she was boasting. She cast around frantically in her mind for a more general, a more abstract remark. 'The scarcity, I have been told, is due to a fall in the temperature of the oceans. Is that true do you think?' She addressed herself to Denis.

Denis pursed his lips before he spoke.

'There is a certain truth in it as far as the western hemisphere is concerned, but it's only partly the cause of the appalling scarcity we are experiencing here. The fact is the foreign fishing fleets no longer fish in the traditional manner. They are not throwing back the small lobsters or even allowing them time to grow to breeding size. Some of those vandals use a modern vacuum method that sucks up everything, fish eggs, the seed bed, everything. They leave the ocean floor as clean as a plate. It's outrageous, but what's being done about it? Nothing. Modern pirates, that's what I call them.'

Maud could scarcely believe he was responding with genuine interest. More unexpectedly she found her own interest was captured, but the smell of fish was now mixed with a strong smell of turbine oil as another trawler pulsed into the harbour, and it was making her a bit queasy. 'Can we walk to the end of the pier?' she asked. It ought to be fresh and blowy out there.'

'Certainly, if you wish, but I must warn you we can't go right to the end. The area around the lighthouse is railed off for security reasons of some kind or another.'

'Denis?' Veronica pulled at his sleeve, quite timidly, in Maud's view. 'Do you think that if we went up even a little way on the cliff walk we might get above the mist, and Mother might glimpse the bay?'

'We can try it, I suppose, if you both feel up to it.'

'I'm game,' Maud said stoutly, seeing he looked in particular at her. To prove it she began, there and then, to pick her way back along the quay. It wasn't necessary to ask the way: the mist had not succeeded in blotting out the cliff which loomed high and dark behind the fish factory, from the door of which, just as she reached it, a bucketful of guts and fish-heads was thrown out on the shingle, and from under an upturned boat, an enormous marmalade tomcat pounced on the offal, snarling diabolically. To give the brute a wide berth, Maud stepped to the left where she had already spotted a path of sorts.

'Not that way! There is a proper path over this way,'

Denis called after her.

Then to her right she did see the man-made path of railway sleepers sunk into pressed clinkers, set at intervals of a few feet to make the gradient less steep. Where she herself had been attempting to go up was only a rut, a runnel made most probably by rain in winter. Or perhaps by sheep? She had seen a number of sheep higher up. It wouldn't be easy to keep one's foothold on the loose shale, yet people must go up this way too because there was litter trodden into the ground as far up as she could see, toffee papers, cigarette butts, rotted orange peels. 'What way do the two of you go up?' she asked of them pointedly.

'This way,' Denis admitted, clearly reluctant to do so. 'It's much shorter, you see, but I wouldn't advise it today.'

'Why not? Because of me? My age? I should imagine I'd be as able for it as Veronica. She never had pretences to being an athlete.'

'Mother! Denis means that it's downright dangerous.'

Maud looked her straight in the eyes. 'It can't be all that dangerous if your husband lets you go up it.'

'Dangerous in this fog he means.' Veronica stood so stubbornly at the foot of the path with her feet firmly planted on the ground, Maud ignored her and went doggedly on upward.

It was heavy going from the start. At every step she took the shale gave way under her feet and several times she had to clutch at tufts of coarse grass that sprouted in rock crevices. The mist had not lifted. If anything the higher up they went the denser it became. And when suddenly a beam from the lighthouse swept over them, it was wan and diluted. It merely flickered over the landscape ineffectually like summer lightning, picking out nothing.

'It's early for that, isn't it?' Denis looked back. 'The mist is not going to lift.'

'But Denis, it's often clear at the top no matter how bad it is down below. That's just intended for the trawlers. Look!' Veronica pointed to the western sky, where the mist had a luminous quality unlike to seaward where the aspect was so wet and gray. 'Please, Denis!' she begged.

The next stretch was less arduous. Now the cliff was sharply indented and the path accommodated to it, twisting and spiralling and making it easier to negotiate. Maud was, at least, less breathless. However, it also ran nearer the edge and was fenced against a sheer fall of what must be hundreds of feet. Fear for the moment took all the good out of the slight respite she'd felt and she felt weak. Below them she could hear the sea bashing against a rocky base. 'Listen to the crash of those waves,' she said, hoping to convey the impression she had halted in rapture at the sound, but she was betrayed in her feint at hiding her fatigue by a loss of breath that caused her to lean back against the paling.

'Don't lean on that!' Denis shouted. 'That's only to keep back sheep.'

Scared by the way he had raised his voice, regardless of her feelings, Maud immediately took her elbows off the paling. There must be a narrow gully down below because the air was filled with a seething sound of wave conflicting with wave. When she recovered her composure she looked with curiosity at her daughter. 'You never had a head for heights, Veronica,' she said.

'I've got over a lot of nonsense,' Veronica said.

What did she mean by that? The enigmatic words made Maud set off upward once again. The erosions in the cliff were now so sharp and narrow and near together the path had become a gyro. She was getting dizzy, and worse still, confused. She could hardly tell now whether she was facing out to sea or inwards to land, except when, weirdly, through the fog a gleam from a buoy or a returning trawler swam into sight for an instant, to be instantly drowned again. A line from *The Tempest*, the play she loved best of all Shakespeare, came into her mind – '*that goodly ship with all the fraughting souls within it*' – but she was in sufficient possession of herself to realize that Miranda was only seeing what Prospero wanted her to see, and in the end when the vessel would set sail again it would be as if there had never been a storm. She called herself to order, but happening to stumble badly it occurred to her that going down could be worse than going up.

'Will we be going down this same way?' she asked involuntarily, before realizing it might be a bit of a giveaway. It was.

'Would you like to turn back now?' Both Denis and Veronica replied eagerly and together.

'Did I say so?' Disdaining to explain herself further Maud pushed on. Mercifully, around the next bend, after skirting a huge rock on one side and the same sheer drop as ever on the other, the path veered away from the cliff altogether and unexpectedly ran, straight as a die, through the middle of a broad and gentle pasture where a full flock of sheep grazed peacefully. For a moment Maud thought they had reached a plateau on the summit, until a massive crag above them made its presence felt by a mortal chill in the air. The path, she saw too, was not as absolutely level as she'd thought at first. On closer view the grassy oasis undulated and seemed to billow like sheets on a clothes line in breezy weather. To the left it sloped softly downward. To the right it rounded slightly upward to form a mound where the sheep, on hearing footsteps, had huddled together.

Denis put his hand on Maud's shoulder. 'From here we could still cut across to the other path and go down that way,' he said, trying to sound casual, and non-committal.

Maud knew she would have to give up. She was dead beat. 'Very well,' she said, with a bad grace, but unfortunately also so loudly that the whole flock of sheep raised their heads as one, and scudded across the path to plunge down the grassy incline. After they disappeared, their hooves, tapping on the shale, rang in the air. Maud listened enviously. Then, encouraged by the ease of their descent, she struck out after them. Oh God! On the slippery windswept grass her feet went from under her, and falling flat on her back she began to slide helpless down the slope. She slid so fast Denis had to throw himself down and grab her under the armpits with such forcefulness in his strong hands that she thought her neck would be broken by the jolt. When he got them both to their feet, Maud could find no breath with which to utter one word of thanks. She tried to show it in her expression and she thought he was aware of it, but he too had got a bad fright and was just as speechless.

Veronica, who had helped them to get up, her face ashen, was the only one who was not speechless. Far from it. 'What is the matter with you, Mother?' she demanded, her eyes blazing, and pointing in the direction Maud had been going to take, where, again, an eerie gleam had appeared, she was livid with anger. Can't you see that's the sea?' she cried, and without another word she herself headed inward. When Denis turned and followed his wife Maud meekly fell into line behind them, taking only what she considered a small, harmless revenge by humming an old nursery refrain.

We joined the navy,
To see the sea,
And what did we see?
We saw the sea.

If Denis and Veronica heard her they displayed no reaction whatever.

When they came to the cinder path, Maud saw that, low in the western sky, the sun, a rosy ball of fire, had burned its way through the mist and fog. One freak ray, rigid as a rod, marked out the pier from sea and land. Packed with trawlers, moored to every bollard, the pier was certainly now full of excitement. Tired as she was, Maud was infected by the animated spirit she was witnessing below. Putting on a spurt she caught up with the other two, and in no time at all they were half-way down. The glow in the sky was fading, fading fast, but as they got to the bottom a string of lights went on from end to end of the pier. And in the fish factory every window flashed with fluorescent light, hard and white like the sparks from an acetylene lamp that strangely stirred the blood. The lighthouse beam had already gained in strength and lit the bay with brilliant blue flashes.

Veronica seemed to lose her grimness.

'Denis, look! There's that caravel again, the one we saw last week. It's back in the harbour.'

'Where?' Forgetting she'd been as good as put in Coventry, and mistaking, only for a split second, two words that after all were very similar, Maud was invaded by memories of the old fashioned hobby horses of circuses long ago. Round and round in her imagination went a carousel of wooden stallions, spanking whites and dappled grey, flaunting their manes of teased rope, one foreleg forever on the ground the other raised for a never-never prance. Bewildered she looked around. She hadn't seen a fair green. Anyway it was late in the year for a circus. 'Isn't it odd to find a sideshow coming to a little place like this in the off season?' She was really curious about it.

'A side-show? What on earth are you talking about?'

Veronica stared blankly at her and as she did, Maud, seeing the caravel for herself, realized her error. Mortified she tried to take refuge in mock innocence.

'A caravel is a merry-go-round, isn't it?' she said.

'That's enough! Stop playing the fool, Mother,' Veronica said quietly, but Maud felt as if she'd been doused with a pail of ice-water. They made the rest of the way down in a silence, made greater by the babel of voices on the pier. Now and then, among them Maud detected a foreign accent which gave her an agreeable illusion of being on the continent, in Concarneau or Fromentin. She would not object at all now to a stroll on that pier. Her sprits rose. But the other two blatantly exchanged another of that special brand of conjugal glances not meant to disclose its meaning to anyone but themselves, whereupon Veronica set her face resolutely towards the ramp that led home, while Denis, excusing himself politely enough turned on his heel and headed the other way.

'I want to have a word with one of the trawlermen,' he said to Maud, who felt it an inadequate excuse for leaving them, but she really couldn't blame him if he was fed up with her.

'Denis! Wait a minute!' Veronica spoke to her mother for the first time since she'd fallen. 'Do you intend to be home for dinner tomorrow night?' she asked.

'Most certainly I do,' Maud was indignant. It was an outrageously rude question. 'I thought I made it quite clear that I would only be staying one night. I know better than to impose myself on anyone, even you, for longer than agreed upon.'

'Oh keep your hair on, Mother. I only wondered if you were intending to go straight home or to have dinner along the way?'

'I intend to leave right after breakfast, if that answers

your question,' Maud said, in spite of not having really settled on any particular time for her departure. No one protested and that didn't escape her notice. Denis just nodded at Veronica in confirmation of whatever they'd confabbed about with their eyes down at the pier. He was already striding away. Maud might have been more hurt if she had not immediately counted her blessings: she'd have Veronica to herself at last for as long as he stayed away. They were no sooner inside the house, however, than Veronica dashed off down the passage to the kitchen to turn on the oven. And no sooner was she back than she dashed off again to attend to some other fiddle faddle. All the same Maud felt pretty good, sitting by the fire with her shoes off and a drink in her hand. Sunk deep into one of the old armchairs, which for all its shapelessness, perhaps because of it, was comfortable beyond belief, she was not even perturbed by the whiff from the dirty oven, allowing herself to condone it by putting it down to the neglect of a former tenant and in no way her daughter's fault. It was hard to altogether ignore the odour though and next thing she knew Veronica was calling her, almost screaming.

'Mother! Mother! Come quick.' Veronica was on her knees in the kitchen in front of a chipped and blackened stove, the oven door of which was pouring out black fumes. 'Oh Mother, I've burnt the dinner. We never use this old stove. We make do with a breakfast cooker, but I was determined to cook something special for you.'

'Never mind, dear. I'm having a wonderful time just being here with you.' Mauds words were pure bravura at that moment as her eyes began to water painfully, but she grabbed the oven cloth from Veronica and took command. Somehow or other she managed to pull out a baking dish she dimly discerned through the smoke and raced with it to the sink. She was more than happy for all concerned when she saw the food itself was not spoiled. It was not mackerel either. She was still further relieved. Nicely browned, a delicious cheesy smelling sauce bubbled and winked around the brink of an earthenware pan. 'Not scallops?' she exclaimed, appreciatively licking her lips.

'I meant them to be a surprise. I know you love them,' Veronica wailed as she got to her feet and gave the oven door a kick. When she stubbed her toe by the violence of the kick, they both laughed. It was like old times. They hurried around the house opening windows and flapping dishcloths to clear the place of the smoke before Denis returned.

The meal when it was served proved excellent, and the wine was not from the carton of table wine Maud had brought: it was chateau bottled, and had been laid on in celebration of her visit. The evening was most enjoyable. Time fled. Maud was horrified when she looked at the clock and saw it was after midnight. 'I had no idea it was so late. You two old fogeys would probably have been in bed hours ago if it weren't for me.' She stood up at once. The others stood up too. And while Denis went around closing windows and doors, Veronica took Maud to her room.

'There's only one bathroom I'm afraid but as the visitor, Mother, you go first.'

'Now, now! No preferential treatment please. I'm not really a visitor dear, I hope,' Maud protested.

'Nonsense.' Veronica piloted her into her room to collect her dressing-gown and wash-bag. Maud couldn't help thinking how infinitely preferable it would be, at her age, to linger over her preparations for the night. But Veronica might almost have been a clairvoyant. 'No need to hurry, Mother. Take your time. Take all the time you want. We'll leave our door open, so we'll hear you coming out.' She bent forward. 'Good night, Mother dear,' she said and they kissed again. Again Maud was disconcerted, made quite self-conscious.

In the bathroom while she ran the taps in the handbasin Maud could hear the voices of the young people, through the wall. The water was coming out in a trickle. It would take ages to get hot. And the pipes were making the oddest knock-kneed noises. Yet a few minutes later when she went to run her bath, the taps in the bath tub gushed out water that was near to scalding, filling the place with steam. Simultaneously with turning the hot tap off and running some cold water she heard a new and deafening noise in the attic as fresh water thundered into the storage tank. That tank must be pint size if it had emptied so fast. She made haste to turn off the cold tap again but it was too late. The hot tap had run cold and the bath was stone cold. All in all there was not much incentive to remain in the steamy little cabinet. The mirror was completely fugged. It might as well have been shrouded in muslin. Deciding not to bother with a bath at all, she pulled out the plug. Good God! What now? The glug glug of the water going down the waste pipe was followed by the most preposterous hiccupping sounds in pipes all over the house. That could go on all night, she thought. Perhaps there was some secret code for preventing it that Veronica had forgotten to give her. Gathering up her clothes, which were now clammy and damp, she wondered why Veronica had thought it necessary to leave their bedroom door open in order to know when the bathroom was vacated. Getting the door to shut was, in itself, an achievement that was not accomplished without a clatter. The wood must have been swollen, or else when she tugged at it, the door had caught on the cracked linoleum.

Out at last, Maud was vaguely embarrassed at having to pass the open door of her daughter's room. She was scurrying across the landing when a dead silence made her glance into the room. To her astonishment, the pair were fast asleep, the light from a naked bulb in the ceiling beating mercilessly down on their upturned faces. Maud stood and stared. Surely she hadn't been that long in the bathroom? Should she switch off their light, she wondered. She decided against interference, but she stood detained at the door by Veronica's extraordinary beauty. That was the way she always lay as a young girl, flat on her back, her heavy hair tumbled all over the pillow. To Maud it was as if, for an instant, the past had been given back to her intact and perfect. Then to her dismay she saw that her son-in-law's head was resting, not on a pillow, but a car rug bundled up like a bolster. He'd get a crick in his neck, for certain. They must only have had three pillows. Oh why, why, had she asked for another, specially when she didn't really want it? Chastened, she tip-toed into her own room.

*   *   *

Next morning, Maud was wakened by Veronica appearing at her bedside with a tray.

'Well? How did you sleep?' Veronica asked, putting the tray down on the bed. 'Mother! I simply cannot understand why you won't stay for lunch. It's ridiculous to dash off straight after breakfast.'

'I simply must go, dear,' Maud lied. She didn't recollect having stated any specific time.

'It's too bad,' Veronica said. 'Denis had arranged to take the day off.'

For what? Maud wondered. The only thing that would have induced her to stay till later in the day, would have been in hopes of a little private session – a little chat – with Veronica when Denis had gone to work. Taking the tray on her knee she made room on the bed for her. 'Sit down and talk to me, dear, while I'm enjoying this,' she said, taking up her knife and fork.

'I wish I could,' Veronica said.

'Oh, I forgot! How stupid of me! You have to get your husband's breakfast. Why on earth did you bring mine first?'

'Oh, we had ours ages ago,' Veronica said, off-handedly. 'I have other things to do though.'

'Like what?' Maud asked, fully aware she sounded prying. Before her daughter had time to answer, the early morning air was tainted by a smell from the dirty oven. Veronica ran for the door. 'I must turn it down,' she cried. 'It's not so bad when the heat is low. I told you we rarely use it except for special occasions.'

What was this special occasion, Maud wondered. They must be having visitors that evening. That, she supposed, was why they had enquired so particularly whether or not she was going early? She looked blankly after her daughter who had gone out and closed the door.

Next minute the door reopened. 'Why don't you lie on in bed for a while, Mother, and have a really good rest. Perhaps you might go back to sleep for a few hours? Veronica gave her a quick smile as she went out again and closed the door.

Maud sank back against the headrail. It wasn't to stay in bed I came all this way, she thought bitterly, and after gulping down her breakfast, she got up without delay. Stripping her bedding and folding it, packing her night things, she fastened her case and left them on the landing outside her door. She was determined to be gone by eleven.

True to her word Maud was at the steering wheel exactly on the stroke of the hour she had planned. There had been several attempts to make her change her mind, but she noticed that her luggage had been brought down and left out in the veranda. Her car had also been backed into the street. This could of course have been from solicitude.

'Oh Mother, it was such a short visit,' Veronica wailed when she appeared at the foot of the stairs, but again Maud registered that her daughter's regret did not prevent her from helping her husband to put the luggage into the car.

As there did not appear to be anything to keep her, Maud stretched out her hand for the keys. 'Well, I'll be off,' she said, as gaily as she could, and she was letting out the clutch when Veronica gave a shriek.

'Oh Denis. we nearly forgot!' Knowing what she meant, Denis raced with her back into the house. They emerged with Denis carrying, bearing aloft you might say, a parcel clumsily wrapped in wads of newspaper.

'A little present,' he said beaming.

What could it be? Fish? What else? Maud shivered. After five minutes that parcel would be a sodden mess. The saturated newspaper would seep water and her car would smell as bad as those trawlers. Her immediate instinct was to be honest and tell them that she really couldn't face fish after her journey. Instead from nervousness she thanked them profusely. 'How thoughtful of you. Put it in the boot,' she said, while privately resolving to stop the car as soon as she got beyond the town, and throw the fish into a ditch.

'Oh Mother. All my surprises went wrong.' Veronica sounded as if she might be going to burst into tears.

Denis put his arms around her. 'Silly girl,' he said, 'We'd have to tell her before she left or she might not find it tonight when she gets home.'

Maud felt like crying too. If only she was arriving now instead of leaving. How had they not known, all three of them, that there were bound to be tensions on a first visit of this nature.

There was nothing to be done about it now though, nothing indeed but for her to depart. Blowing two kisses for them to distribute as they saw fit, she drove away, going slowly, as she had promised.

Outside the town she found she was still going slowly, because she was thinking over the disappointments of the visit. For a split second she thought of turning the car and going back to say she had behaved badly, had been over-sensitive, if not downright stupid, and that she'd like to come again soon. Next time would be so much better, things would go much smoother. Then, remembering the early days of her own short-lived marriage, she realized the young pair would already have scampered back into the house, glad to be alone again, and talking about other things, things entirely removed from her visit. Finding she was now travelling at a snail's pace, and that to one side of the wood, there was a grass bank, topped by a high hedge of thorns, it occurred to her that this would be as good a time and place as any to deal with the fish. Without a qualm, she stopped the car and took their well-meant present out of the boot. Admittedly, she was vaguely aware as she took it out that the newspaper wrapping was neither cold nor wet, but this fact did not register fully until it was too late. Raising her arm, exerting all her strength, she sent their parcel flying over the hedge into the field beyond. With a gasp she heard something break, and peering through the

close-knit thorns she saw fragments of crockery protrud-
ing from the newspapers, and, yes, yes, unmistakably a
lobster claw. Appalled, she looked around for some way to
get into the field, but the hedge was as impenetrable as a
thicket, and she could see no road-gate. She stood helpless
on the lonely road and then she began to laugh. There was
nothing for it but to get into her car and continue on her
way.

Coming up out of the hollow of the port, on to the main
road, high above sea-level, Maud glanced into her rear
mirror.

The morning sun shone full on the small port, on bay
and shore. As for the cliff that had been so sinister and
menacing the previous evening, it was as if it had been
struck by a magic wand and all its crags and rocks grown
over by verdure, and, what was more, a verdure blonded
by sunlight.

Maud stopped the car once more and got out to look
back.

The stillness of it all! The waves that must be incessantly
breaking on the shore, and the tumultuous waves that must
still be dashing violently against the base of the cliff and
sending their spray heaven-high into the air, seemed, all, all
to have been stilled. From where she stood they appeared
like a painted frieze, fanged but static, in the way that
mountain cataracts in Connemara cascaded thunderously
downward drenching the roads with spume yet seemed,
when one looked back, from even a short distance away, no
more than a veining of white marble in the black stone.

Maud was chastened by what she saw, and she felt there
was a portent in it for her, but if she was to fulfil her
promise to travel slowly, she'd better not loiter.

As well as that, it had suddenly entered her head that in

her hurry leaving home she might not have closed the French door that led into the garden. It was unlikely that any intruder would venture into the house, but a stray animal could do untold damage. And thinking of damage, she began to wonder if she would be able to find a casserole to match the one belonging to Veronica that she had broken. It was almost certainly part of the dinner set that had been so proudly brought into use for her benefit. If she could find a matching one, she could bring it down next time she went to see them and with luck they'd never know about the small calamity that had overtaken the lobster. In any case, she felt sure that if they did find out they would be amused at the catastrophe. Everything would be so different on her next visit. And of course they were right, it was far too long a journey for an overnight visit at her age. Indeed if she did not gather up a bit of speed, it would be dusk before she got home, because now, of course, she would certainly have to stop along the way for dinner.

A Marriage

James changed down into first gear when he saw the old spaniel waiting for him under the crab-apple trees half way up the driveway. He had been slowing down in this way every evening lately to bolster up the poor dog's delusion that he could still outstrip the car.

Time was when the spaniel could hear the car coming along the public road and be waiting down at the entrance gate. How James used to rejoice in his frantic barks of welcome.

The drive out of Dublin was long and tiring after a hard day's work at the university, although James never conceded this to his colleagues. To them he swore that the extra effort was well worth while for the satisfaction he felt when he reached the gate of the farm and knew that in a moment he would be in the middle of his own fields. His jangled nerves were immediately calmed by the broad expanse of unfenced pasture under the immense dome of sky. Like the sea, the flat Midlands seemed to make manifest the dominance of the heavens over the earth. Back in the car again after closing the gate behind him and having taken a deep, deep breath of the sweet untainted air, he was ready and eager to give his full attention to the spaniel and always entered wholeheartedly into contest with the dog to see who would be first to reach the inner gate which separated the grazing land from the grounds around the house.

When the dog was young it sped alongside the car, skimming the ground like a swallow, its tail-featherings streaming in the air, stiff as pennants. In those days James had to keep tooting the horn to hoosh cattle out of the way. Nowadays the heavy beasts paid little heed to the car edging slowly between them. They merely raised their heads in mild curiosity and went back to peacefully cropping the grass.

This evening when an enormous bullock stood stock-still right in the middle of the drive, James had to nudge it with the bumper before it lumbered off after the others. Clear of the cattle James still drove at a snail's pace to give the dog a change to recoup its flagging energies and gain a few yards' advance on the car.

The poor dog was getting old. It might soon have to be put down. In spite of a feeling of infinite sadness James had to smile to see how foxy the old fellow was still. It had managed to get directly in front of the car so James couldn't possibly go any faster without danger of hitting it. 'Good dog,' he called out, touched to see how the old dog risked turning his head, his rheumy old eyes pleading for recognition of being in the lead, yet in those eyes there lurked a look of guilt as well, for having put his master at a disadvantage.

When they finally reached the second gate, and the driveway opened into a wide gravel sweep in front of the hall door, the dog must have decided that, at this point, it could, without loss of face, let the car proceed unaccompanied to the garage. Panting heavily it lay down at full stretch.

No longer encumbered by his escort, James swept smartly around to the service end of the house, giving just a cursory glance at the kitchen windows in case Emmy might be looking out to wave at him. But the kitchen windows were coated with steam and he could see nothing within. She was probably at the other side of the house setting the table in the small study where they usually took their meals now that the last of the children was grown and gone.

In the garage, James took his briefcase from the passenger seat and was about to reach over to the back seat for the armload of messages from the village shop, which, without respite, he had to pick up for Emmy every evening since they'd come to live here in the country. This evening, however, he was overwhelmed by such a great urge to stretch his limbs, unimpeded by packages, and to take another breath of the cool evening air before going inside that he only took out his briefcase and left the messages where they were. He could come out for them later if anything was urgently needed. Wearily he thought of the desk in his study here at home. It was more cluttered than his desk at the college, because here he had no secretary to deal with trivial things and file them away out of sight. Here too he was not spared phone calls even though he was away all day because Emmy conscientiously took all calls that came for him and jotted down the name and number of the caller, promising he would ring back. As likely as not there would also be a number of pencilled scrawls left for him by one of the workmen with regard to a job the fellow had felt free to leave undone at quitting time and to which James himself often had to attend. And invariably Emmy herself had an accumulation of chores laid out for him, a fuse to be replaced, a drain to be unclogged, a drawer unstuck. God only knows what she'd want him to do. Perhaps because he was really deadly tired this evening a mean thought came into his mind. Was it to ensure that he'd have ample time to attend to those behests of hers that she made such a fine point of having their meal ready on the dot? Not that he ever baulked at attending to something urgent, or really minded pottering round doing some silly, fiddling and totally unnecessary task, as long as it didn't take up the whole evening. It would have been ungrateful in view of the excellence of the meals Emmy always provided. It just seemed a bit much to go straight into the house immediately he arrived, to bolt back into the burrow as it were, and lose the last precious minutes before the light faded, the time he could have savoured some enjoyment from his land. Except for Saturdays and Sundays, he was properly walled-in from dawn to dusk, only quitting the house for the car, the car for the office, which he seldom left even at lunch time, just grabbing a sandwich and a paper cup of coffee from the slot machine in the basement of the Students' Union. Then when he was released at the day's end the routine was merely reversed and he went from office to car, car to house, house to bed. Ah well. He got out of the car, slowly; his legs were stiff after the drive. He glanced again at the fugged up windows of the kitchen. In spite of the perfect weather out of doors, rills of water ran down the inside of the glass panes. And seeing that Emmy's car was still in the exact same place where she had left it the last time she had been out in it, untidily parked, one wheel up on the grass verge, he was irritated. He'd have to park it properly or it would destroy the grass edging. She would never do it, never. He was about to put down his briefcase and do it there and then but force of habit made him nervous about letting the case out of his hand so he decided to open the door to leave it on the hall table. But as he put the key into the lock, James, to his surprise, found himself doing so as noiselessly as possible, you might go so far as to say stealthily. And although he was only vaguely conscious of it, he closed the door behind him as gently as if it was the door of a sick room. Only then did he realize that he was not going to bother with her car, he was going to go over and lean for a few minutes on the fence of the paddock where the children's ponies used to be put out to grass and of which little use was made nowadays. He only intended to stay out for as long as it would have taken to park the car, but when his eyes travelled beyond the paddock to a small beech wood that marked the north-west confines of his property and separated it from a pretty streamlet that was a tributary of the Boyne, he thought he had never seen the view so enchanting. The upper branches of the trees were tangled in skeins of the late sunlight. It was a heavenly sight and it seemed to give a benediction to his little escapade. For he knew then that he was going to stay out a little longer than he had originally thought. He was going to get over the fence and walk across to the wood, or at least go far enough to see if any of the young green leaves had broken from their pale pink sheaths and begun to unfurl. Emmy would surely understand? Maybe with a bit of luck she might not have heard the car draw up, although, now, crossing over to the fence he no longer cared that his feet made a loud crunch on the gravel until, startling him violently, Emmy appeared, coming, not from the house but from the garden.

'James! I didn't hear the car.' The contrite note in her voice made James feel like a criminal. On her arm she had a garden trug filled with globe artichockes which she held up to show him. 'Did you ever see anything as perfect, James? Such a blend of purple and green. They're a different variety from the all-green ones we have been growing. These are supposed to be more succulent. They're certainly exquisite looking, aren't they? They remind me of those porcelain ones we went so near to buying in Paris.' She stopped abruptly. 'Years ago, do you remember?'

Oddly James did remember the pretty ornaments they had been sorely tempted to buy, but which he had in the end judged far too expensive. Even before she mentioned them just now he had had a vivid recollection of staring at them in the shop window near their hotel on the Quai de Bethune. He and Emmy were on their honeymoon at the time. Had she forgotten that? Did she think it was on one of their later holidays? Somehow he thought she remembered. She had paused so awkwardly in the middle of a sentence, as if on the brink of saying something different. If so she had displayed a subtle tact for which he felt grateful. For some time now he had a real wish to feel more deeply for her, but she didn't make that easy with her unbelievable carelessness about her appearance. As on every other evening, she was still in her old gardening skirt and her hair was pulled into an untidy knot on the nape of her neck, with wisps escaping to either side. That soft, loose way she wore her hair used to be very attractive, but now that her hair was grey she really ought to make an effort to control it. He had always respected, and shared, her belief in being natural, but perhaps now that she was getting on in years, she ought to have something done about her looks like other women. Her hair was streaked with so many shades of grey that, combined with her grey dress and old grey cardigan, she was more like a pigeon than a woman, but here his heart smote him when he thought of how beautiful her hair had been when she was young. That raven hair! People were forever remarking on it, althogh the banality of their compliments had often infuriated him. Only dyed hair was jet black. Emmy's hair had the living darkness of a bird's wing, with flashes of blue and green and even glints

of gold. James sighed and brought his mind back to the
artichokes. 'They're beautiful, Emmy,' he said sincerely,
but Emmy, who had found a slug in one of the leaf axles,
had forgotten her own question. He reached out to take the
trug from her and dispose of the slug but he was truly
impressed by the artichokes. 'We ought to exhibit these
next year at the Trim Show,' he said, to compliment her.
Did he fancy it though, or did a shadow pass over her face.
Perhaps she was thinking of all the fruit and flowers she
had grown over the years which he had never before
bothered to praise, much less suggest exhibiting, the little
tomthumb narcissi, the miniature roses, and rarities like
sisyrinchum striata, which grew for her as prolifically as
weeds, to say nothing of vegetables like these artichokes,
which she tried in vain to give away to the local people,
who relished only cabbage and turnip. He was trying to
think of something to say that might give her pleasure
when he saw she had shaken the slug out into the palm of
her hand.

'Oh James! Look. It's putting out its tiny horns at me.'
She was enthralled by the little creature, but when he put
out his hand to take it on his own palm and look closely at
it, she stepped back from him. 'You're not interested in it,'
she said, and to his astonishment tears had come into her
eyes, although she quickly winked them away. Really she
was getting very unpredictable of late. He stared down at
the spaniel sprawled at his feet, but the dog was looking at
him with eyes filled to the brim with a love so total it made
him uncomfortable. More than ever he longed for a few
moments alone.

'Emmy. Would there be time for me to take a short stroll
before dinner?' he asked, not caring any longer if he upset
her. He was determined to enjoy the last of the sunlight.

'Are you feeling alright James?' she said looking anxiously at him. She held up the artichokes again. 'These are for tomorrow night, not for tonight,' she said, obviously alarmed in case he might think she still had to cook them. When he assured her he was alright, that he only felt the need for a breath or two of air, to his dismay she left down the trug.

'Why don't I come with you?' she said. 'There is something I've been wanting to say to you for some time. I turned off the cooker before I went out, so nothing will burn. We'll have plenty of time to take a little walk if we hurry.'

'Very well,' James had to give assent. Daylight was fading fast. In the small copse the trees were swathed in a mist as blue as the blue mists of distance. Only the pinnacle of one tall conifer glowed gold.

'We'd better be quick,' Emmy said, taking his arm, but she had turned towards the garden. Firmly James freed his arm and throwing a leg over the fence he held out a helping hand to her.

Amazed Emmy stood and stared after him. 'Why are you going that way? There's a pane of glass missing from one of the cold frames. I thought that if you could take the size of it this evening – I have a tape measure in my pocket – you could get a new pane cut in the city tomorrow.'

Vaguely James wondered was that what she had wanted to talk about. If so he was not going to bother with it now. 'Listen Emmy, I haven't been over in the woods for weeks. I had a great longing to go over there this evening. You needn't come if it's too far for you.' He saw she hesitated, but it was only for a second. Then she allowed him to help her over the fence.

'I warn you we won't be able to see much,' she said, but

in the field, where they had to walk in single file along the narrow headland because the grass was high, she got more enthusiastic and prodded him in the back. 'Faster, James, I just remembered that the workmen told me a tree fell over here last week. I forgot to tell you about it. If there is enough light we could investigate the damage.' Although it meant wading in the long grass she came abreast of him. 'The men said a lot of branches had fallen into our field. We ought to get them gathered up and drawn into the yard so they can be sawn and split for firewood.' In her eagerness she actually went ahead of him and was almost running forward. Then suddenly she stopped and faced him. 'Oh James, isn't it a shame to think — '

James stiffened. It didn't seem possible that she was going to treat him to the dismal dirge she normally reserved for visitors, but not noticing anything amiss, she was babbling happily on. 'Such a pity,' she sighed. James coughed in hopes of not hearing the rest of the lament.

Years back, when they'd first thought of buying the land, which then had no house on it, they were both under the impression that the wood which sloped down to the river was part of the property. It was a keen source of regret to them to find that the belt of trees belonged to the neighbouring estate. James had seen several practical disadvantages in not owning the wood and the access it gave to the stream, apart altogether from its loss as an amenity. All the same he allowed the sale to be closed and went ahead with plans for building his house. He was probably still under the misapprehension that he could eventually acquire the wood. But the neighbouring property proved to be entailed and its owner a ward of court, young enough to outlive Emmy and him, or at least outlive their ambitions. Every time they visited the site they deplored their loss. All the same he bought the place and managed to oust his disappointment from the forefront of his mind. Emmy, however, whose regrets had been based on nothing more than a romantic notion of clearing a glade and planting it with bluebells and wild anemones, had never lost her sense of deprivation and actually succeeded in keeping his alive.

As they got nearer to the wood James saw that she was right about a tree having fallen. A lot of branches lay scattered in their field. She was wrong, though, in thinking those branches would be any use for firewood; they were too rotten and soggy, but that did not mean that they could be left here. They would have to be carted away and dumped. He stretched up to try and see over the unruly hedge, guessing that in the wood other trees had probably fallen, although the general neglect made it hard to see much.

'You'll have to write to the trustees again, James,' Emmy said.

'There's not much point in that, as you ought to know,' he said impatiently, 'They'll only send the letter back to their steward and you know what he'll do with it!' James couldn't help being curt because he, too, was now deeply dejected. The wood was well on the way to becoming a swamp. It would encourage rats and attract swarms of horse flies. With difficulty he scrambled up on the bank and managed to make out something of the mess beyond it. Yes. At least five or six trees were down, lying where they fell alongside the rotted trunks of others blown down through the years and never removed. The remains of those dead trees, coated with viscid lichens and sprouting nauseous fungus, would foster all kinds of vermin. Lice! He shuddered. Dusk was rapidly giving way to dark, but as his eyes grew accustomed to the lack of light he saw that on the bark of a badly decayed log just underneath the hedge a coil of worms wriggled in a loathsome embrace. And without looking further he knew of old that deeper down, nearer to the stream, however dark it got the stark limbs of long dead trees, peeled bare by friction with the branches of strong self-sown saplings, would gleam with sickly whiteness, clamped as they were for eternity in the fork of the young trees still living, still green.

'James,' Emmy called up to him. 'We could at least get the briars slashed on our side of the bank. Why don't we get that done?'

James frowned. She was right again. It was essential to have their own side of the hedge breasted. He could have no quarrel with that suggestion. It was Emmy's passion for getting things done that jarred on him. He jumped down from the bank.

'We'll do nothing of the sort,' he said. 'At least the brambles screen us from that ghastly sight. Come on. Let's go back to the house.' He whistled for the dog. 'Where is he?'

'Where do you think? Down in the river. He'll amble up covered in mud.' Emmy was obviously nettled by his brusqueness.

When the dog did appear, James saw at once it had not been in the river, not even near it. He patted it on the head. Then, with the old dog plodding after them, they made their way home. There was a chill in the air and by then it was pitch dark. Nearing the house, James instinctively produced his key to the front door.

'What's wrong with the back entrance?' Emmy strode towards the kitchen door. Hastily James followed her, but when they got to the door the spaniel was about to waddle happily inside in front of them until Emmy shot out her foot and blocked its way. She was too late though and the old dog sidled past her. 'Damn, damn, damn!' she said.

'What's the matter now? He wasn't in the river,' James protested. Then he looked down at his own feet and saw that his shoes were wet with dew. The dog's shaggy paws would have been soaking, and indeed he could see that the tiled floor of the passage was already patterned with wet prints. To James those familiar trefoil paw marks were positively lovable. They'd dry out almost immediately, or else they could be taken off with one swipe of a mop. Why did Emmy have to make such a fuss about it? He wondered if her real grievance was that the old dog had lately taken to waking her in the night, whimpering to be let outside. She had been complaining about it for some time. Perhaps he should bring the matter into the open, here and now. Emmy, however, had rushed into the kitchen and seized a mop with which she began to attack the floor. He took the mop from her, but she was not placated. She returned tight-lipped to the kitchen to engage herself with the battery of pots and pans which were apparently essential for what she called 'dishing up' the dinner.

James, who could, if the need arose, boil an egg, considered this 'dishing-up' – what a word – to be a purely female ritual, so after he'd mopped the floor, he took example from the dog, and passing straight through the kitchen to the study he sat down to wait for the meal to be served. The old dog was already flat out in front of the fire, dead beat. James stared down at the old chap with compassion. If Emmy was being wakened by it every night, as she claimed, it would certainly have to be put down. Quite honestly, he believed Emmy was exaggerating the problem. How was it he never heard the dog, not a sound, never, never? Granted he was a heavy sleeper, as was only to be expected after a day's slogging in the college, but he did not sleep the sleep of the dead. Why didn't she wake him? He'd get up and let out the animal. He wouldn't grudge the few seconds it would take. In his opinion the poor old thing deserved top marks for not peeing on the floor. 'Good dog,' he said again. But the dog was fast asleep.

'I'm ready, James.' Emmy was alerting him to the fact that she was bringing in the cover dishes. He sprang to make place for them on the table. The food smelled good. There was no mistaking her gift for serving up a delicious meal in record time.

After eating, James felt better. As far as he could judge so did Emmy. The old dog too seemed to be having pleasant dreams to judge by the happy little yelps that escaped it now and then. In spite of a bad start the rest of the evening was uneventful and a glass or two of red wine made both of them sleepy. By ten o'clock they were yawning, and when the last chime of the clock in the hall died into the stillness, they stood up together with the unspoken accord of the long-married to attend to the securing of doors and windows, the raking of the fire and the innumerable other preparations for the night that Emmy considered of vital importance.

James dutifully went though all the motions with her, until she began to spread protective newspapers over some pot plants on the windowsill in case of a late frost. He felt he could stop short of that. 'I'm going on up ahead, Emmy,' he called from the foot of the stairs.

'Aren't you forgetting something, James?' On wings of fury she had flown after him.

Seeing that her angry glare at him took in the dog as

well, James realized he had not put it out to relieve itself, and benefiting by this neglect it was just about to make a try at repeating its earlier success and squeezing between his legs to get up to its basket on the landing.

As Emmy had done earlier, he tried to stop it with his foot. 'Oh, no, you don't!' he said playfully, and dragging it back by the collar with one hand, he opened the hall door. 'Come on. Out you go, good boy,' he said. 'We don't want you waking us at cockcrow.'

'Us?' Emmy's look was blistering. Smarting under her look James planted a soft kick on the dog's rump to accelerate its exit. But Emmy had glanced out into the night. 'I didn't know it was raining,' she said slamming the door shut. 'Do you mean to say you would have let it out in the rain to get its paws wet again?' Puzzled, the old dog looked up at James, who was himself confused.

Who'd have thought the weather would change and the night turn out so badly after a glorious afternoon? He did hear rain, now, heard it falling, falling heavily and gurgling in the drains. He looked from the dog to his wife. 'What will we do?'

'I suppose it's a choice between two evils,' Emmy said.

'Evils?' James raised his eyebrows. 'For God's sake try to keep a sense of proportion. What do you want me to do? Shoot the poor bugger?' He was joking of course, but Emmy didn't take it as a joke.

'All I ever wanted was to discuss the dog with you, to know that you are aware of what I have to endure. Take for instance the way he keeps me awake. It's not the dog I blame. It's not the dog's fault that I'm easily wakened, just as it's not your fault that you sleep like a log. I suppose like most men who have to go off to work every morning, you tell yourself that as a woman I can make up the lack of sleep by taking a nap during the day, which of course, is something I have never done in my whole life. Oh James, James, I cannot rid my mind of something you said a few months ago. You've probably forgotten, but I never, never will. You hurt me to the quick. You said that maybe I only dream that I am awake. James, oh James, how could you have said such a thing?'

James did vaguely recall saying something of the sort, but he had no idea she'd taken it to heart. He was about to protest, to explain that he'd read it somewhere, that he didn't really believe it, but she silenced him.

'You not only said it, James, but I know why you said it. It let you off the hook. It absolved you from having to worry about me. Mind you, I am prepared to admit there may be some truth in your allegation. People who are lying awake in the night for hours and hours could probably drop off now and then for a few seconds, and when they wake, they could possibly be a bit confused about how much or how little they slept. Take last night for instance. Last night, for once, I did get to sleep fairly fast, but I woke again almost immediately thinking I heard a bark. I sprang up and went out on to the landing only to find the damn dog fast asleep. It was so fagged out it didn't even give that little stir of its tail it gives to let us know its aware of us. Do you see what I am getting at, James? I am admitting there may be a borderline between consciousness and unconsciousness, but you, *you* implied that I was not honest, you implied – '

'Emmy!'

'I'm not finished, James. Please listen to me. You don't listen you know. Time and again I've tried to tell you that I'm often wide awake when the yapping starts. I'm not always wakened by the dog. But it's against the law to let a dog run loose in the dark so after that I cannot go to sleep again. I have to stay awake deliberately until sun-up.'

Sun-up? James winced. Another of her idiotic expressions, but then her whole argument was idiotic. 'For God's sake, Emmy, the old dog is long past savaging sheep.'

'That's what you think. Well, I have news for you, James. When daylight comes at last, and I let him out, do you know what he does? He hares off over the fields – to chase rabbits, if nothing else. He doesn't make the slightest attempt to lift his leg. I know. I've watched him. It's not for that he wants out, nor for that he whimpers and wakens me. And that's not the worst of it. If, by chance, after I do get back into bed I happen to doze off for what's left of time before your alarm clock goes off, that damn dog is under the window yapping to be let in again. You have him spoiled, James. You made a proper nuisance of him.'

'Hold on there, Emmy. You seem to forget I'm away all day. If anyone is responsible for the dog it's you.' Thinking he had scored a hit there, and perhaps put an end to the topic, James backed up two steps of the stairs, but he could not ignore the entreaty in Emmy's eyes.

'Oh James, what is the matter with us?' All rancour was gone from her voice. 'I know we can't expect things to be like when we were young, but surely we ought to feel some gratitude for what we once gave each other, gave freely and generously.'

James was absolutely astounded. What rubbish was this? He had never gone in for affairs of the heart even before marriage, much less afterwards, but he felt this was the way a woman would talk if she thought a man was slipping away from her.

'We're no different from other couples of our age,' he said.

'Is that so? Oh James! When we were young would it have satisfied you to think we'd end up like other people?

'End up? What do you mean? Are you planning to leave me or are you trying to persuade yourself that I am going to leave you?' He expected a real row to break now. He was wrong. Emmy's face had softened and she answered quietly. 'We could be nicer to each other, James. We could have taken better care of our love.'

That was better. James relaxed.

'Well, we can always try again, dear,' he said and he reached out a hand to suggest she, too, would come upstairs. He was really deadly tired all of a sudden and when they heard a creak of wicker on the landing overhead and realized that the old dog had benefited from their bickering to slink up to its basket, they both had to laugh. James firmly took her hand in his.

She hesitated for a second. 'There was something I wanted to say to you but I suppose it can wait until morning,' she said.

'Of course it can,' said James.

*   *   *

To James the most ridiculous thing about this particular squabble was that Emmy was the first to fall asleep that night. He himself had barely placed his studs in the tray on the dressing-table where they would not roll off on to the floor and had thrown his soiled socks on the carpet, prior to taking a clean pair for the next day out of his drawer, when he became aware of a strange silence. Emmy was asleep. Looking at her he derived a brief-lived amusement from the irony of this, before returning to his preparations for the morning. Unknotting his tie and selecting another to go with the fresh shirt he'd decided upon, he stepped out of his trousers and carefully spread them across the back of the slipper-chair on which they both left their clothes at night.

As on every other night, Emmy's clothes were neatly folded on the seat of the chair, covered with a small square of pink satin, edged with tarnished silver fringe she had cherished since her girlhood. By day it did double-duty as a holder for her nightdress. When they were first married those modest mementoes of her days in a convent school used to amuse him. He used to tell her she was as fastidious as a cat although in spite of teasing her like that he paid homage to the fact that she had never shown any false prudery. Tonight, however, he looked away in disgust from that pathetic scrap of pink satin, knowing the discoloured garments it hid, shoulder straps fastened on with pins, split seams, torn yolks, and gussets mended with big black stitches of tacking-thread put in as roughly as rivets in a plank of wood. She really was the limit. It was not amusing, he told himself, as he got into his pyjamas and dropped into bed beside her to wait expectantly for the magic wand of sleep to strike.

To his distress it did not strike. He was an unbelievably long time lying awake and although beside him Emmy's breathing was so soft he could hardly hear it, following upon her grousing about insomnia, it affronted him. After a time he began to think it was her breathing that was keeping him awake. If so how could she expect him to believe that on other nights he could stay asleep while she tossed and turned on the other side of the bed. Wasn't it well known that all human beings altered position many times in the course of a night, thumped their pillows, hunched the blankets over them or threw them off. Yet Emmy expected him to believe that he never as much as stirred even if she put on her bedside light a dozen times. She even claimed that she often got up and went downstairs, made a pot of tea and brought it up to bed on a tray while she read for hours. That was too far-fetched for anyone to believe. Tonight her claim to be a poor sleeper rang pretty hollow. He was tempted by the mind not the flesh to move closer to her and determine by a nudge if she was really asleep, but he couldn't stoop that low, although it might have relaxed him to talk with her for a while. As things were, he was getting so tense he was beginning to believe he would not sleep a wink all night. Then a disturbing thought occurred to him. What if this sleeplessness became a nightly business? Nonsense! He was not the kind of person to let anything get the better of him. After all, there were plenty of sedatives on the market. For that matter, if Emmy really and truly suffered from insomnia why didn't she take something, some tablets or pills to combat it? It was no use her saying she disapproved of drugs. Up to now he disapproved of them too, but another night like this would put things into perspective for him. At their age, anyway, what matter the habits they formed? Indeed if he remembered righly she had once tried tablets of some sort but she held they had not worked for her. More nonsense! She had not found the right brand, that was all. She should ring her doctor and insist on a different prescription. Better still, perhaps he ought to give her doctor a tinkle in the morning and have a private word with him. He'd thought of doing this once or twice in recent months, but never at a proper time. The idea usually occurred to him when he was already snowed under by a million other commitments. The thing to do was to make a note in his memo pad, but that was in the office. He'd have to get up and scribble a note on a scrap of paper. Oddly

enough before he had time to do that, James had fallen
asleep.

★　　　★　　　★

The next thing James knew it was morning. At least the
bedroom was no longer pitch dark. Had the alarm on the
clock gone wrong? He was bewildered. Outside a small
bird gave a chirp, but it was a solitary note that need not be
taken for a herald of day. It could not possibly be time to
get up. Feeling as tired as he did, he could by no means have
had his full quota of sleep. Fleetingly he thought of waking
Emmy but the memory of their conversation before going
to bed inhibited him. He closed his eyes once more. After a
few seconds he cautiously opened one eye again and saw
that the curtains were outlined with light. That might of
course mean that the curtains were not properly drawn and
that it was a bright moonlit night. He opened the other eye.
The things on his bedside table were faintly visible, except
for the clock, which stupidly was at an odd angle, the
clockface just out of his range of vision.

James lay as still as stone, hardly daring to breath until it
occurred to him if Emmy was still in the bed beside him he
ought to be able to hear her breathing, gentle as it might be.
Perhaps she'd gone down to let out the dog? Perhaps for
once its bark had disturbed him?

Lying in extreme discomfort, it occurred to James that
in the rigid position he was trying to maintain he might
easily get a cramp. That would be a nice kettle of fish. He
decided he'd better risk putting out a hand to feel if Emmy
was still in the bed. Then curiously compulsively he
recalled the first night they had lain in one bed together.
They didn't sleep much that night but next morning he

could have sworn that, even sunk in sleep, he was aware she was in his arms. Emmy, too, swore that all night long she never fully lost consciousness of him.

For months after their wedding night, they lay locked in that close embrace. Naturally in time, particularly if the night was a hot or muggy one, they drew apart by mutual consent before they settled down to real sleep. Even then, they woke to find their arms entwined.

Understandably Emmy's first pregnancy interfered with their sleeping habits. She often got uncomfortably hot in bed, and could only endure one blanket, whereas he never found two enough at any time of the year.

During that first pregnancy of hers, he used to lie, quite literally, on the edge of the mattress, aware of her as ever all night, except that by now his awareness was painful and he was jittery in case a jerk of his knee or his elbow might hurt their unborn child. Emmy used to laugh at him and assure him that the child in the womb was well insulated. He found this hard to believe until the child first leapt in her womb. After that it was him who got prodded by its embryonic elbows and heels.

Even then, even with the bulk of the unborn child between them, they woke at the same moment each morning, and the looks they gave each other in those waking moments were as intimate as a caress.

Oh, the magic of those days. It was a long time since James had thought about that enchanted time. Money worries and the stress of academic life had cast their shadows over him and diminished his recollection of the past. It was not just, as it might be with other people, that in their young days it was their youth itself that had cast its spell over them, because his own life had been dismal enough until the day he first saw Emmy. Their eyes had met in the middle of a lecture he was giving to first-year students, and from that instant he had been transported into a new world. Although the girl was sitting in the back row, it was exactly as if she had touched him with a fleshly torch. Yet when he tore his eyes away he was panic-stricken because it seemed then that she was thousands and thousands of miles away, at a distance from him he could never bridge. Daring to look down at her again he could still hardly believe she was still there, and then in spite of bench after bench of students between them it seemed as if all others in the room had dissolved into thin air and he and she were close enough to hear each other's heartbeats.

He knew he had to speak to her and it had to be that very day because it was the end of term, and the long summer holidays were beginning next morning.

On a feebly trumped-up excuse he waylaid her in the corridor after the lecture. When he learned she was leaving that night for three months in Innsbruck, he threw discretion to the winds and asked if he could write to her.

Oh those letters! He hardly knew or cared what she wrote, he was so intoxicated by the sight of her handwriting, by the very feel of the envelope. Once, when he'd lost the key to the postbox at his flat, and had to squeeze his hand into the box and fumble around to see if there was any mail for him, he had had the most extraordinary sensation when his fingers touched a letter from her, although the envelope was no different from any other.

Oh where did it go, that magic? To think that for years he had not noticed it was gone. For years he had complacently accepted the substitutes of good living, companionship, affection, loyalty and perhaps above all care, good care, and had only lately faced that these things never made up for the delirium of first love.

Emmy, on the other hand, had acted all along as if each step of their marriage had been what she had expected. Quite early in their marriage it had surprised him to see the ease with which she threw away flowers that were only a day old and not really withered. That now seemed to him in some way symbolic. She gathered up the flowers seeming happy to have something else besides tea leaves and the outer leaves of vegetables to put on the compost heap she had made at the end of their garden, and in which she had soon begun to take as much pleasure as he took in the flower beds. Of course that was when they were still living in the city. Down here on the farm her compost heap was of such huge proportions and he himself was often glad to avail himself of a few tractor loads of it to put on a crop of potatoes or mangels.

Women, evidently, accepted nature's ordinances more easily than men, but to give Emmy her due she never expected any pretences of gallantry from him. How they both despised those fatuous old fools who hobbled to open doors and pull out chairs for their dreary wives, holding their coats for them to back into like a mare backing into the shafts of a cart. He had never for a moment been unfaithful to her, even in thought, it was just that he hungered for the bewitchment that had lured them into each other's arms, while she had taken its disappearance for granted. She had made up for it by the joys of maternity and after the children were grown she had concentrated on the practicalities of their life, the meals for instance. But suddenly James recollected another small incident that happened on their honeymoon. They were visting Lake Como and were crossing the lake on one of the little steamers from Bellagio to Cadenabia, when there had wafted down upon the water from the fabulous gardens of the Villa Serbelloni a scent so piercingly sweet their breath was taken away by it. Emmy had identified it and had said a strange thing.

'Wild cyclamens! To think how tiny they are, and what millions of them it must have taken to produce a scent strong enough to reach us out here on the water. Think of all the poor deluded bees that must have been lured here for such small reward.' Then she had laughed. 'Nature ever was a deceiver,' she said. Surely that was a strange thing for a young girl to say on her honeymoon? And now, years and years afterwards, it occurred to James for the first time, that perhaps she was not as complacent as he'd thought. Whether that made things better or worse, however, he could not at that moment say. He blinked his eyes. Had he dozed off again? The room was now blazing with sunlight. Outside this time not one but hundreds of birds filled the air with their clamour. Violently James flung back the bedclothes and grabbed the clock afraid it had stopped, when suddenly Emmy came in the bedroom door, fully dressed and carrying a tray of tea.

'I turned off the alarm, James. It can't be good for you to be galvanized into activity morning after morning by that ear-splitting sound. Also you may remember that I said I had something to tell you last night, but the time didn't seem right.'

James glanced impatiently at the clock. Did she think her timing was any better now? 'Look here, Emmy, can't it wait till this evening?' He put one leg out over the edge of the bed to reach for his clothes but she was between him and the slipper-chair. He supposed he'd better let her get it off her chest whatever it was she wanted to say, let her give him the gist of it maybe and then agree to discuss it when he came home if it merited discussion. 'What is it?' he asked.

This time it was Emmy who looked at the clock. 'James, would you consider just for this once, telephoning the college and tell them you had to stay home today?'

'Are you in your right mind? Say what you have to say now and be quick, Emmy. I'm listening.' He was glad to see he had flustered her.

'I don't know where to start,' she murmured. But she did. She launched right into it. 'Do you remember the day last week that I went to Dublin?'

She went so seldom he did of course remember. Moreover he could pinpoint it as the day she parked the car on the grass.

'Well, I'll tell you why I went. It was to see the doctor.' Ignoring the start he gave, she went on. 'That dear old doctor who was so good to us all when we lived in the city.'

The doctor? James was stunned. He fell back against the pillows. Such a rush of blood came to his head, his sight blurred and he thought for a moment blood had gushed into his eyes. He could not see her distinctly. 'Oh God Emmy. What's wrong? How could you have kept something like that from me? What did he say? What is the matter with you? Oh why didn't you tell me before now?' He wanted to stand up and take her in his arms but he was inhibited by the disloyal thoughts he had been harbouring against her lately. Oh God, what a fool he was! If anything were to happen to her, it would be like the amputation of a limb. Again he wanted to put out his arms to her but this time he pulled himself together. He must not panic, or at least he must not let his panic show. 'Look here, Emmy. You should have told me if only so I could have brought you to a top man. That old ass may have been kind to us – he was, very, very kind, but he must be as old as a bush now, a thousand light years behind the times – probably hasn't a clue about the advances made in medicine. Of course I'll stay home today. I won't bother ringing the college either. But you haven't told me what was the old fool's diagnosis?' Distraught he looked at her and their eyes met. James was momentarily distracted. How young her eyes had remained. They were the eyes of a girl. How was it that they never looked into each other's eyes nowadays? Maybe that was where love took refuge when the rest of the body was drained of the power to evoke it. 'Oh Emmy, Emmy, what is the matter? Tell me. Tell me.' His eyes still clinging to hers, he went to clutch her to him.

Gently Emmy pushed him away. 'I must explain something, James. It was not to consult him about myself I went. I went to make an appointment with him for you.'

'Me?' James was first dumbfounded, then outraged. 'How dare you interfere in my life, attempt to interfere I mean.' He glared at her and under his glare Emmy recoiled, recoiled and indeed crumbled.

'Forgive me, James,' she said. 'I didn't think you'd take it this way. Truly I didn't.' Then she grew more confident. 'I simply felt I had to do it, you've blinded yourself for too long to the strain you've been putting upon yourself with that long drive back and forth to the city, specially in recent years since you can't be said to be in the first bloom of youth. Furthermore, it's me who has been taking the brunt of it. You've become almost unbearable, snapping my head off every time I open my mouth. You've been irritable, contemptuous, on edge all the time. I suppose it could be said I was acting in my own interests almost as much as in yours. Quite frankly I think you should retire, either that or sell this place and move back to the city.' Seeing his face darken still more she backtracked a bit. 'The doctor did not suggest that, by the way. He'd have to have a look at you first. A good rest might be his solution. He might merely prescribe a tonic. Oh James, think of what life would be for me without you.' Tears came into her eyes.

James was still stupified by her temerity in having taken the step she had, but all the same he was struck by the coincidence of her saying almost exactly what he had been thinking with regard to her. And of course he knew there was some truth in her words. Hadn't he been feeling more tired than usual in the past few weeks? And it never did a person harm to have a medical check-up at any age. He relaxed slightly.

Emmy of course was quick to take advantage of him. 'I think you ought to retire,' she said getting her words in quickly before he could say anything else. 'You needn't pretend that we cannot afford a cut in our income. In any event you will be eligible for two-thirds of your pension, won't you? As for me a slight drop in our standard of living wouldn't be the end of the world – one car instead of two – that sort of thing – compared with the pain of seeing our relationship going to pieces more and more each hour.' Suddenly she began to sob.

'Don't cry, Emmy,' James said. He knew he should be glad of her concern. Right or wrong, wasn't she the only one who was concerned about him. The children? He wondered about them for a moment. They loved him but their own husbands and wives, to say nothing of their children, were quite rightly their main concern. 'I'm sorry I shouted at you, Emmy, but there can be no question of my retirement. It would put the college in too awkward a position, although a rest, a short holiday might be a damn good idea. That could easily be arranged. For that matter we needn't go away. A few days at home here would be fine for me. I don't need a doctor's prescription for that, my

dear.' He spoke abstractedly because he realized it was not
only a few years since they had gone on a holiday, it was so
long since they had taken as much as a day off, he couldn't
remember the last occasion. 'Look here, Emmy,' he said
impulsively, 'Of course I won't stay home today as long as
there is nothing wrong with you. I won't stay the whole
day I mean, but I can ring and say I'll be late if you'd like to
come to town with me. How about that? You could fool
around until I was free and we could go and have dinner
somewhere decent, give ourselves a treat, eh? How about
it?'

'That would be nice,' Emmy said vaguely. 'But I'll only
go on one condition, that you come to the doctor. I'm sure
he would see you without an appointment under the
circumstances.'

Circumstances? What circumstances? 'Out of the question.' He didn't mean to snap at her. He regretted it and he
was glad she didn't seem to mind. She probably wouldn't
have come with him anyway, he thought. She was in her
old gardening clothes and she hadn't displayed great
enthusiasm, just a polite acknowlegement of the invitation.
On second thoughts it had not been such a good idea from
his point of view either for various reasons. For one thing
he'd feel obliged to meet her for lunch and today that really
wouldn't suit. Against that again, if she came he might take
her up on the remark she'd made about selling her car. That
might still be a sensible course of action, she so rarely used
it. However, they could discuss that in the evening. 'Well,
how about it? How long would it take you to get ready?' He
knew he sounded lukewarm but she didn't seem to notice.

'Another time, James,' she said. 'When you've had time
to digest what I said, I'd enjoy an evening in town.'

Relieved, James none the less had an intuition that he

ought not to leave her without some effort to make her happier. For both their sakes. He cast around in his mind for something else to say and quite by accident he lit on a funny story. 'Do you know, Emmy, your going to the doctor about my supposed ailments reminds me of the woman who went to confession and after she'd told her own sins, she branched out into a long litany of her husband's sins. Do you know what the confessor did? For her own penance he gave her one Hail Mary and for her husband's sins he told her to say the whole fifteen mysteries of the rosary.' That did the trick! She laughed.

'Goodbye dear,' she said and leant forward and gave him a little quick kiss. Free finally to go, James reached out once more for his trousers, unaware that Emmy had taken them up and was absently folding them. 'Be careful,' he cried. Too late! From the hip pockets a shower of small coins and keys and other odds and ends rained down on the floor and rolled away in all directions, most of the coins taking cover under the bed, the chairs, the chest of drawers and the wardrobe. James' earlier outrage was nothing to the rage that enveloped him now. 'Why the hell did you do that ?' he demanded as he went down on his knees and scrabbled about under the bed to retrieve above all his car keys and enough small change to tip the car park attendant.

Biting her lip with remorse Emmy went to help.

'Don't bother!' he sneered. 'Just tell me why you do these idiotic things. Is it to annoy me?'

'I don't know,' Emmy said lamely, desisting from giving any more help. But she did know and suddenly she blurted out her reason. 'I suppose it's because I've always loathed, right from the beginning, the way you spread your trousers out on that chair, with the fly open, it's so – ' she searched for a word, ' – so obscene. They look as if – '

He didn't let her finish. 'Get out of my way,' he yelled and in his hurry to get dressed he hardly noticed whether she was in the room or not until he heard her footsteps on the stairs.

In a few seconds he was ready to go, but as he finished knotting his tie he went over to the window and saw with mixed feelings that Emmy was outside going towards the garden. She would undoubtedly have left his breakfast ready but he didn't intend waiting to eat it. He leant out of the window to call out goodbye. She didn't hear him. She was obviously going to turn over her precious compost heap because she had a manure fork in her hand and her feet were stuck into a pair of his old boots with the laces taken out. As long as she had that compost heap he needn't pity her for companionship.

Next minute James was speeding off down the drive. The old spaniel watched him go. It was really incredible the instinct dogs possessed. The spaniel never made any attempt to accompany the car in the mornings. It just looked sadly after it, knowing its master would be gone all day. After James had opened the inner gate, driven through, shut it again and was back in the car, a jumble of associations reminded him of another dog they had had earlier in their marriage. It was a poodle and very cute. They all loved it, particularly the children. One day it had a fit and after a few recurrences they got the vet, who when he came early next morning, said there was only one humane solution. He did the deed on the spot, and was gone before they knew where they were. They didn't have time to feel sad, however, because a small crisis developed. The children could not be let see the dead dog. It would have to be buried at once. The problem was that the workman was not due for an hour and James was already

late in leaving for Dublin, so he and Emmy would have to
bury it. Then that problem became magnified. There had
been a black frost during the night and the ground was
hard as iron, neither with spade nor pickaxe could James
break it up.

'There's only one thing we can do James,' Emmy said in
desperation hearing sounds that indicated the children
were awake, 'We'll have to bury it in the compost heap. It's
the only place the soil will be soft enough to dig a proper
sized hole.' There was no gain saying that. It was what
they'd had to do. The thought had occurred to him but he
had been reluctant to suggest it. Emmy had surprised him
but a few weeks later she really took the wind out of his sails
by her lack of squeamishness.

'When do you think we'll be able to use the compost?'
she asked. What she meant was when would the dog be
decomposed? Then the funny thing happened. Well, it
wasn't exactly funny, it was grim. The workman they had
at the time was an old man named Ned. That evening Ned
was waiting for him at the gate when he came home.
'There's something the Missus might like to know,' Ned
said. 'She can soon start using that compost where you put
the dog. I had a few minutes to spare today and I thought
I'd get a spade and see what progress he was making.
Nicely sir. He's doing very nicely. All the hair is gone and
the skin is beginning to go on his back. He'll be nothing but
bones before the summer.' It was certainly a bit macabre
but how they laughed, he and Emmy, at the old man's easy
attitude to it all.

James had by this time reached the road-gate but
thinking back to that incident and to other moments in
their early years on the farm had made him feel very
strange. Their quarrel this morning had upset him. He

wished with all his heart that he had tried harder to persuade Emmy to come with him. He had a notion to go back to try again, but he simply couldn't summon up the energy to turn the car around. He sat on at the wheel. Emmy's words about his health must be preying on his mind. He remembered how scared he was when he thought she was ill, and how moved he had been when he had looked into her eyes. With a deep sigh he roused himself and opened the car door, but instead of getting out he closed his eyes and let his head rest on the back of the carseat, when he felt a warm breath on his face and a warm body pressed against him. Emmy? The crazy thought that she'd followed him was dispelled in an instant when a hot, wet tongue began to lick him, lick, lick, lick, not just his hands but his face. It was the old spaniel. What the devil had got into it? What had made it come after him? How did it know he was not already miles away? 'Get down! Get out!' he ordered. The dog took no notice. If anything the licking became more insistent. James roused himself sufficiently to try and push the animal away with his hands, only to find that the old dog had more strength than him. It went on licking him and licking him and at last James gave up the struggle. He closed his eyes and his head fell back.

The Face of Hate

Johnny knew the other boy only by sight, but he hated his white, Protestant face and his sedate, Protestant step.

It was 1957 in Belfast. Johnny was sixteen.

The two boys passed each other every morning of the week, except Saturdays and Sundays, at the same time, and almost exactly the same spot. It galled Johnny to think the little Protestant was then within a stone's throw of the grammar school, while he himself had yet to get across the city to St Mary's. He never managed to be in time even though he rattled hell out of his old bike. He slunk into class every morning with what one of the priests called punctual tardiness.

Saturdays were different. There was no school that day, although he still had to serve mass and do a paper round. Yet, when the alarm clock went off, he could luxuriate in the knowledge that when he'd get home he could have his mug of tea in comfort with his feet under the kitchen table.

Sometimes of a Saturday afternoon, he'd catch sight of the other fellow coming home from rugger, carrying his football boots in a calico bag like a sissy. Once when he pointed him out to his pal Jer, Jer asked how he knew it was the same fellow. It was Jer's conviction that all Protestant kids looked alike, all pasty faced, all with blazers, and all with school caps set straight on their pates like pudding bowls. Few Catholic kids could afford a blazer, and those who had caps wore them down over one ear in a shamefaced sort of way.

Johnny used to think no Protestant kid ever had to wear hand-me-downs, but one night when he and his father were sitting in the kitchen with her, his mother put him right on that score.

'There are poor Protestants as well as poor Catholics,' she said.

'Not in Belfast,' his father butted in, from where he sat hugging the range, nursing a sore head after a day spent in the pub. The shipyard had laid off another two hundred men and not one Protestant among them.

'Yes, even in Belfast,' his mother said stoutly. 'You only think they're well off because they're thrifty and take care of their clothes. The clothes that come out of a Protestant jumble sale are as good as new. I've heard they get them cleaned and pressed before they give them away and don't even cut off the buttons. I've heard they polish the boots and put in new laces, and wash and darn socks so's they won't be unpleasant for others to handle. You wouldn't get many Catholics to show that consideration for the poor of their parish.'

'Ah,' said his father peevishly. 'Have sense. What's poverty in a Catholic is parsimony in a Protestant.' He stood up and kicked off his boots by pressing down on the broken uppers of one with the heel of the other, scattering mud all over the clean floor. Then stepping carefully over the bucket of soapy water that was left unemptied so the front steps could be swilled down last thing, he went up to bed without a word of goodnight.

Johnny looked at the muddy marks on the floor and then down at his own boots with their knotted laces and toecaps bleached white by wet and weather.

'I'll do the doorstep for you, Ma,' he said, but she snatched up the bucket and he saw she was looking regretfully at his jacket. The day she bought it she'd bought a card of buttons as well, but she'd never got round to sewing them on.

'Do you know something I heard the other day, son? In Germany, boys as well as girls are taught to sew. Would you believe that? Ah well, never mind. You'll be getting a brand-new suit next year when you're sitting for your examination. I've my heart set on it. I was not going to tell you until it was paid off, but I made the down payment on it today.'

Johnny's face lit up. She'd been a good mother to him always, as she had been to Sheamus when his older brother was still at home. Never, even in their poorest days, had she forced either of them to wear articles of women's clothing, the way other mothers did. That very day he had seen a little kid in primary school wearing a green coat with a flared tail to it. Thinking to amuse his mother, he started to tell her, but it didn't make her smile.

'The poor child. I hope you didn't let on to notice, son,' she said. 'His poor mother was probably at her wit's end trying to keep him warm in that draughty school. I suppose the heating will soon be shut off now the worst of the winter is over?'

'Shut off?' Johnny had to laugh. 'It's been out of order since January.' He held out his fingers to show his chilblains broken and running, and as he did, he thought of the smell of blistering paint from overheated radiators that wafted out the open door of the grammar school as he pedalled past it, his hands fastened by frost to the handlebars of the bike. He could almost hear the hot water rumbling and gurgling in the pipes like human guts. But his mother was harking back to the child in the girl's coat.

'That poor child is likely fatherless,' she said, shaking her head sadly. 'Not that your own father ever has a stitch of clothes fit for passing on to a beggar after they come off his back, God help him. It's true he spends all he can lay hands on in the pub, but he makes no bones about wearing the same suit of clothes year after year until it falls off him in tatters.' She sighed again, and changing the heavy bucket from one hand to the other, she opened the street door. Looking up and down to see no one was passing, she sloshed the sudsy water out over the doorstep. Johnny remembered a time when, like her neighbours, his mother used to scrub the doorstep every Saturday night and whiten it with lime. That custom, like many another, was given up when curfew was imposed on the city. When she came back and left down the bucket, she closed the door. 'Tell me, son, would you happen to know the name of that little boy you were telling me about? It might have been one of Larry Lardner's children, God be good to him, the youngest one. I saw that wee Lardner child myself one day wearing a cardigan a bit gaudy for a boy. It must have been sent home by one of his older sisters from England because I remarked at the time the good quality of the yarn. Oh, son, son, that wee fellow was only an infant in his mother's arms when his father was shot dead at their own hall door in front of them all. I was at the father's wake, and although the shroud hid the bullet holes, I could get the smell of singed cloth. Ah, well. There's no use talking about those things. It's only keeping the bitterness alive.'

Johnny couldn't let that pass.

'It isn't us that's keeping it alive, it's them, the Protestants. You know that, Mother.'

His mother made the sign of the cross. 'May the Lord

have mercy on the dead, no matter who they are, or what they did.'

To please her Johnny crossed himself. He knew it must have gone against the grain with her to have made even that one reference to the atrocities that were the main topic of talk in other houses, talk to which the children listened avidly, and repeated next day in the schoolyard. Jer Murphy's mind was an armoury of terrible tales about things done up in the Divas hills to fellows belonging to illegal organizations, fellows like Sheamus. But he didn't want to think about things like that when he was going to bed.

'Goodnight, Mother,' he said, reaching for the flannel rag that hung on a string over the range, to wrap it around the hot brick she always insisted on his taking to warm the bed, although it only made his chilblains sting like nettle rash. He was startled to see there was a second brick set to heat. 'Are you expecting Sheamus, Ma?' he cried. It was several months since his brother had dared come home.

His mother's face went ashen and she sprang to her feet, and looked in terror at the thinly curtained window. 'Ssh, ssh,' she cried. 'I know nothing. It's only that I had a queer feeling he might steal in tonight for a wee while.'

Her face flushed, and it was as if she was transfigured to a girl again. Then, catching up the poker, she nudged the brick off the range and into the coal hod and pushed the hod out of sight. 'May God forgive me. If anyone came to the door that brick would be a cruel giveaway.' She sank back wearily on the chair. 'Go to bed you, Johnny, will you, like a good boy. I have a few more chores to do before I turn in.'

Johnny knew what that meant. She'd sit up half the night in case his brother might appear. She often took these notions, and never seemed to learn from disappointments. There was nothing he could do about it. Her hopes and fears were inextricably tangled together. Well. Better that maybe, than her to lie tossing and turning, listening for a sound of gunfire, thinking her own son could be the next to take a bullet in the belly. Johnny wrapped up his brick and went to bed.

*   *   *

The next day was the Twelfth of July, a public holiday, and in spite of what their parents felt toward the Orange Order, Catholic kids often had a great day of it. Even when he was in primary school, Johnny used to go up to Donnegal Square with Jer and his pals to watch the parade, sneering silently during it and jeering loudly on their way home through the empty streets. Lately, it wasn't such fun. Now Jer and the others were almost as tense as their elders. As he jumped out of bed and ran downstairs, Johnny half hoped it would rain. Then, when he went into the kitchen, he was astonished to find that his mother, for once, was not down before him. The blinds were not up and the range was not lit. Looking into the coal hod he saw the brick was in it, ash grey and cold. He let up the blind. It was a fine day, and, as he scorched off down the street in the sunlight he was soon whistling. Pedalling home he was whistling louder still, and when he reached his own street and saw the brass knocker was shined, he knew his mother was up. All was well.

In the kitchen his mother was on her knees scrubbing the rungs of an upended chair, but she got up at once, and he knew by the smile on her face she'd managed an egg for his breakfast. The kettle was boiling on the range, and on the mantleshelf there was a big brown egg.

'Where is the yard brush, Ma?' he asked when he'd eaten. He wanted to do something for her.

'It's in a place you won't find it, son,' she said smiling again. 'Go off out for yourself into the fresh air, it's little enough of it you get.' She glanced at the window where a dazzling line of sunlight ran along a crack in the glass. 'It's a lovely day, thanks be to God.' Setting the chair back on its legs, she knelt to scrub the seat of it, but after a minute she stopped and rested her elbows on it as if it were prie-dieu in the chapel. 'What are you going to do with yourself today, son?'

'I don't know,' he said lamely. 'I'll see what Jer and the others are doing.'

His mother pursed her lips. She looked up angrily at him. 'You know as well as I do that you'll go to watch the parade. Small wonder the Orangemen prance around the streets when all the Catholics in the city turn out to gape at them. They'd soon give up parading if there was no one to admire them in their sashes and their bowler hats, banging drums like babbies.'

'It's not to admire them we go, Ma,' he said coldly.

But this too she knew. It was of this she went in mortal dread. 'Oh son, I wish you'd stay away and set an example to the others. A single stone idly picked up out of the gutter and fired at one of them Orangemen and the next thing fired could be a shot.' She stared down at the suds in the bucket that were winking out one by one, and he knew she was thinking of Sheamus. To please her he thought he'd get his books and study for a while anyway, and he started to hunt around for them on the window sill, the mantle-piece, the floor. 'Sheamus always kept his books in the one place,' his mother remarked absently.

Johnny looked up. He felt sure she was comparing the two of them, comparing them to his disadvantage. She was probably thinking that even if Sheamus came to no harm, he had thrown away his only chance of a decent career. Sheamus had had brains to burn, but Johnny felt his mother had no such confidence in him, although the priests were putting him in for the same scholarship Sheamus had thrown away. Yet the old priest who took the Latin class had made a strange remark lately. He said that fellows with application often did better for themselves than fellows who only abused the brains that God had deigned to give them. Just then, he found the books. They were under a clutter of old racing calendars belonging to his father. His mother stared at him.

'Ah, Johnny, isn't it a pity it's not this summer you're sitting for the scholarship instead of a whole year from now?'

'You wouldn't wish that if you were in my shoes, Ma,' he said quietly.

She saw the sense of that. 'You're right, son. Amn't I the foolish woman wishing the years away. It's only wishing your life away. Keep on the way you're going, keep out of mischief and God will reward us.'

Johnny stuck to his books and only went out with Jer and the others an odd time, although his mother distrusted the others more and more. On the other hand Sheamus, during one of his rare forays home, had put in a good word for Jer.

'That Jer has guts,' he said, in one of the awkward silences that were liable to fall on them sometimes as they all listened unconsciously for a sound in the street. 'He's a good kid. His heart is in the right place.'

Johnny could hardly believe his ears when his mother

turned on his brother. Usually, when Sheamus slunk home, she did her best in a few minutes to lavish a lifetime of love on him. But now her face flamed with fury. 'Leave his heart out of it,' she cried. 'No more than yourself, I don't suppose he knows why God gave him a heart in the first place, unless to pump hate into his veins.'

Sheamus only laughed and tried to chivvy her up. 'Come on, Ma. You and me always had our differences over affairs of the heart. You didn't take it well if I as much as lifted my eye to a bit of a skirt of a Sunday after mass, even if it was only one of the O'Grady girls down the street, one of those poor dried-up skins that will never get a man.'

Johnny was going to laugh until he saw their mother's face.

'God help all mothers,' she said. 'I thought in them days you were a bit too young for that sort of thing.' She hurried over the last words as if she had expressed herself too crudely. 'I thought then, God pity me, that you were going to lead a normal life. I didn't know you were saving yourself up to be a target for the RUC.'

Sheamus' visit that night ended badly. When he went away, Johnny knew their mother would lie awake until all hours, eating out her heart at having made them all miserable.

*　　*　　*

Slowly the summer wasted and went the way of all summers. And when the next summer came, it was not like other years because at the end of it Johnny would be sitting for the scholarship, and he had been given extra study to do at home during the holidays. He spent a lot of time at his books. His mother had insisted he give up the paper round

though, and the priests let him serve a late mass, so he had a
good lie-in most mornings. After breakfast, when he'd sit
down at the kitchen table with his books in front of him, his
mother used to go around on tiptoes so as not to disturb
him, and even his father, when he'd got up at noon, took
himself off to the pub earlier than usual, not to disturb him.
The new suit was paid for in full and hung in the cupboard
awaiting the big day.

Saturdays were a bit different.

'You've done enough reading all week,' his mother
would say, especially if it were a sunny day. Giving glory to
God for all His blessings, she'd tell him to go out and enjoy
himself. 'There's no use breaking down your health, son,'
she'd say.

Then, one week in mid-summer, there was a bit of
trouble in the street. The RUC had raided two neighbours'
houses including O'Grady's, and although nothing was
found, everyone's nerves were on edge. Unfortunately,
that week the Twelfth of July fell on a Saturday, and the
first thing Johnny noticed after his breakfast was that his
mother had cleared a space on the table and spread out his
books. She had set a bowl of flour at the other end of the
table to make a cake of bread, and the range was stoked up
for baking. The kitchen was murderously hot. Compared
with the heat inside, even the sunlight outside seemed cool.
Seeing him gazing out, his mother ran over and rattled up
the window. Then she rushed over to the yard door and
flung it open.

'That'll let in a nice breeze,' she said, as if he were going
to spend the day there. Was she playing innocent, he
wondered? She couldn't but know he'd be going to the
parade. He was no longer in the know about all Jer's plans,
but he had a feeling there might be more in the wind this

year than just gawking. Everyone in the street was ratty over the raid. They would not do anything bad, maybe only let off a few squibs or firecrackers. All the same, they'd be counting on him going with them.

As a cool, fresh breeze blew though the kitchen, Johnny opened his book. He'd stick at the work for a while. Pouring over the book though, he was soon engrossed. It was his mother who was fidgety. She went back and forth continually from the table to the range before she at last settled down, poured a cup of water into the bowl of flour, and began to stir it with a big wooden spoon. Then, plunging her hands into the bowl, she furiously kneaded the dough. But she must have felt guilty. 'You ought to be out in the sun, I suppose,' she said at last.

'Ah, that sun is too bright to last. It'll probably be pouring rain before long,' Johnny said, thinking to forestall an inquisition. 'There's no use making any plans in this rotten country.'

His mother scraped the wet dough off her arms before she answered.

'It won't rain,' she said dully. 'I sometimes think the Orange Lodge must control the weather in Belfast as well as everything else. Oh, son, it's a wonder to me you have nothing better to do on a nice, fine Saturday, than stand about in the streets breathing in the dust stomped up by those goms of Orangemen. If I was young again, or your poor father for that matter, it's off up to the hills we'd be on a day like this. Yes, every Saturday in summertime all us young people used to set off up to the Divas. And when the evenings got short we'd walk out along the Lagan to Shaw's Bridge. And not only us. The foremen in the shipyards always walked their greyhounds out along the Lagan.' Johnny was impressed. He'd never been up the hills unless in a car, and he'd never gone far along the Lagan. He'd have thought the riverbanks were all built up with houses and factories. He looked at his mother. She was talking very excitedly. 'Sometimes, even in winter, we'd have such a wish to get out of the dirty city we'd go down to the quays, just for a smell of the sea. Were you ever down there?'

'I was, Ma. I was down there a few times with Sheamus.'

As if struck by a thought that had not before occurred to her, his mother was silent for a moment, staring down at her floury hands. 'I suppose you miss your brother too,' she said. Then she looked up and said a most extraordinary thing. 'At your age, son, and with your looks, it's a wonder to me some nice girl hasn't put her eye on you. I'll bet there's plenty would be proud to be seen out walking with you of a fine Saturday.' Johnny blinked. He was three years younger than his brother, and he hadn't forgotten how his mother had clamped down on Sheamus where girls were concerned. Ah, she was cunning. She didn't believe, she never did, that he would get the scholarship, and she was afraid that if he failed then there'd be nothing to stop him going the way Sheamus went. But he recoiled from the idea that she would make use of a girl, any girl, as a decoy to keep him at home. She didn't know him as well as she thought. He couldn't look a girl in the face without going through agonies. Once recently, when he got a puncture on the way home from school, and had to walk and wheel the bike, he saw one of the O'Grady girls standing at her door, and rather than pass her, he turned back and went round the block to enter the street from the other end. He wouldn't have minded if it had been one of the older ones, but it was the youngest of them, and she was the one he dreaded. She seemed to be always standing in the doorway.

Even when he whizzed past her on his bike, he often felt she
was staring at him as if she were deliberately trying to make
him feel a fool. People said she was the brainy one in the
family. She played the fiddle too, and Jer said she'd have
got a scholarship to the London Conservatory of Music
only she dug with the wrong foot. She wasn't bad with her
old fiddle. He'd heard her himself scraping away at it nights
he'd pass the house after dark when the blind was down.
But suddenly his mother came closer to him and broke into
his thoughts. 'That's another injustice the Protestants
inflicted on us, the worst of all,' she said. 'By not
distributing jobs fairly they made it impossible for us
Catholics to get married until it's too late for us to grow
together in the bonds God intended, and have the size
family He meant for us.' She lowered her voice and there
was an intimacy in it he had never before known her to
show. 'I was thirty before your father and me could afford
to get married. That's why I only had you two boys.
Protestants of course, no matter how much money they
had, would never think it a loss to have only two children.
They see to it they don't have any more. They never
hesitate to interfere with nature. May God forgive them.'

Her nearness suddenly irked Johnny.

'In a few years' time we'll be doing the same as the
Protestants,' he said. 'They're better educated than us,
that's all. If you ask me, the priests and bishops have ended
up making paupers of us.'

His mother's face went ashen.

'Where did you hear talk like that? Who are you aping?'
Jerking around, knocking over a chair in her anger, she
turned her back to him.

Johnny looked in misery at her rigid shoulders. Now, he
wouldn't be able to go out at all, or, if he did, the image of

her ashy face would follow him wherever he went and take the good out of the whole day.

'Ma, I didn't mean to speak bad about the Church,' he said. 'I was only repeating what the Protestants say about us. It's only old guff.' When she didn't stir, he raised his voice. 'If you ask me, Protestants are too mean to have kids.' Then remembering something funny a crony of his father's had said one night when he had been sent to assist the two men home from the pub, he trotted it out. 'Protestants are so mean they wouldn't give you the steam off their piss.' Too late he realized that the old crony was stinking drunk when he'd said that. For a moment his mother was struck dumb by what he'd said. Then her glance flew to the statue of the Sacred Heart on the shelf over the sink and blessing herself, she soundlessly moved her lips. She was asking forgiveness for him from the statue.

That was too much. Johnny opened the door leading into the street, but all desire to go out had been drained from him. Instead, he leaned back against the jamb of the door and stared into space. Behind him, he heard his mother open the back door. She had evidently produced the yard brush from wherever she'd hidden it, because next minute he heard the sound of it. It had so few bristles left, she might as well have been beating the ground with a stick.

At first, standing in the doorway, Johnny gazed out vacantly, but when two girls appeared at the far end of the street, his attention fastened on them. They looked as if they were parting, but instead they remained standing beside a lamppost, talking and laughing. The lamppost was between him and one of the girls, so he couldn't see her face. The other was the young O'Grady one.

At sight of the girls, Johnny was mildly agitated, but so long as they stayed at the far end of the street, he felt safe to stay at his own door and take stock of them. Eileen, that was the name of the young O'Grady one, had now put her arms around the lamppost and was swinging out from it as if she were waltzing with it. Silly twit. The other one had a fiddle case, but she'd left it down, and now Johnny saw she was Kitty Lardner. She was probably too early for a music lesson and the O'Grady one was keeping her company. What were they gassing about, he wondered? What did girls gas about anyway? They were always at it. He looked away in contempt.

A few minutes later when Johhny looked back, the girls were still yapping away. A pair of gas-bags. The Lardner one now lifted up her fiddle case, but then she left it down again and put her arms behind her head like she was leaning back against a pillow, instead of standing in the public street. Twits. Both of them. Had they nothing better to do than jabber, jabber, jabber? If it weren't for his mother, he'd go back into the house. They weren't worth wasting time on. The Lardner one was skinny, and her hair was short and oily. The O'Grady one was at least good looking. He remembered Sheamus once saying she was the pick of the O'Grady crop, and that she wouldn't be left on the shelf like her sisters. At the time, that made him snigger, but now, remembering his mother's words, Johnny felt sort of sorry for those older girls. They weren't bad looking either. Wasn't one of them at one time sweet on Sheamus? He tried to remember. Perhaps they mightn't be on the shelf if fellows like Sheamus and their own brother weren't on the run, when they ought by rights to be ... Johnny pulled himself up short. Ought to be what? He must be getting soft in the head, he thought. He looked around to find something that might take his mind off the girls, and overhead, perched on a telegraph wire, he saw a row of small birds. As he looked at them, one small bird took wing and flew away, followed in a moment by another. Then three more took flight. The line was steadily diminishing. Were they departing at random or mustering to some secret call-up? Now five, no, six took off together, followed soon after by another loner until finally only two little birds sat on the wire. Johnny decided that when those two flew away, he'd go inside and not stand any longer like a gom in the doorway.

'What on earth are you staring at, Johnny Mack?'

Johnny nearly jumped out of his skin. Eileen O'Grady was standing beside him. How had she come up the street without his knowing? He thought his knees would go out from under him. Why had she passed her own door? 'I was only looking at the birds,' he mumbled, confused and shamefaced. Remembering the day it was, and that she was Sean O'Grady's sister, he felt he had to offer some explanation for being at home. 'I was going to bring books back to the library only it's a public holiday,' he said. Then he threw in a small lie to make weight. 'They're overdue. There'll be a fine to pay on them.'

To his relief she seemed to find his explanation acceptable.

'You are the clever one of the family, aren't you, always reading, the one they say will get on in the world, always studying.'

Johnny reddened with pleasure at the compliment, but he felt he had to disclaim it. 'I don't know about that,' he said. 'What's the use of any of us addling our brains when there'll be no job for us after we leave school. Maybe it's different for a girl,' he added quickly when she seemed crestfallen.

'It's no different at all,' she said. 'I've given up the fiddle. I'd get nowhere with it. I'm taking sewing lessons in the tech, instead, night classes.'

'Do you mind much?' Johnny asked timidly.

'Not much,' she said, 'I wouldn't object to being a dressmaker if I lived anywhere else but Belfast, where I'll be doing nothing from one end of the week to the other only mending old rags of clothes that ought by rights to be thrown out. I'll be turning frayed collars, relining baggy skirts, and putting false hems on smelly old coats and dresses. I know what it will be like, because I give my mother a hand. Look.' She held out her index finger. It was etched with needle pricks. But it was at her fingernails that Johnny stared; they were like small pink shells he'd seen on the seashore at Killard once when he went there on excursion organized by the school. Ashamed of his own dirty nails, he put his hands behind his back and tried with one fingernail to prize out the dirt from under the others, but his nails were stubbed from biting them and the black was lodged below the quick. He gave up. Anyway, she wasn't looking at him. Her eyes had a faraway expression. 'I'd have left here long ago if it wasn't for my mother, knowing the dread that comes over her in the night if she hears a patrol car coming down our street.' Johnny nodded. He knew all about that.

'Where would you go, if you could. Is it to England?' She gave him a scathing glance.

'You must be joking. Honest to God, it's no wonder the English despise us, with everyone in Ireland thinking England the only place in the world jobs are to be got.' She pursed her lips in annoyance, like his mother did when she was threading a needle. But when his mother did it, the blood went from her lips and they wrinkled up, while Eileen O'Grady's lips got fuller and she looked as if she were going to blow make-believe kisses up into the sky.

'Where would you go, so?' he asked, curiosity getting the better of his shyness.

'Ah, I don't know.' She was suddenly dejected. 'If I ever do get a chance of going, I suppose I'll end up in England like everyone else.'

'Well, you're not taking off today, anyway,' Johnny said quickly, hoping to cheer her up. Her face did brighten.

'Can I ask you something, Johnny Mack? If the library was open would you really be going there? Or were you just standing here mooning?'

For the second time Johnny recalled where her O'Grady sympathies lay. Did she too expect he'd be going up with Jer to Donnegal Square to watch the parade? 'If you want to know, I had a row with my mother,' he said recklessly.

She seemed surprised. 'About what?'

'I used a dirty word,' Johnny said, and he felt his ears and neck flush painfully. To his surprise, a little smile fluttered around the girl's mouth.

'What did she say to you?'

'Nothing. But she looked at the statue we have over the sink and she blessed herself, and I knew she was apologizing to it.' As he told her, his feeling of outrage came back. She only laughed.

'Oh, Johnny. All mothers are alike. One day when my brother used a bad word, my mother snatched the muffler off his neck and wound it round the head of our statue so it wouldn't hear.' That was a good one. A broad grin came on Johnny's face, but the girl's voice had grown harsh. 'As if God would listen to anyone in Belfast, Catholic or Protestant, with the evil they both do in His name. Take my advice, Johnny Mack, and don't worry about your mother. It's a pity the library isn't open. It must be nice in there. I often saw you going up the steps and I wished I had a ticket.'

'Oh, a ticket is easy to get. You've only to ask for one at the desk and get it signed by a teacher.' Johnny couldn't get over her noticing him. Then his enthusiasm got the better of him. 'Would you like me to get a ticket for you? I'd get it for you on Monday.'

'Thank you. Some day, perhaps,' she said civilly, and Johnny came down to earth again. There was an awkward silence. Then the girl broke it. 'It's a nice day, isn't it?' she said, perhaps casually, but it made Johnny feel good. He looked up at the sky where a few clouds had gathered, soft and fleecy, making the sky look bluer.

'Do you know what my mother told me before she got mad at me? She told me that when she was young, people thought nothing of going up the Divas of a fine Saturday. It must be lovely up there today,' he said. The girl looked unbelieving. 'Yes,' he said, 'and when the days got short they used to walk out along the Lagan as far as Shaw's Bridge. Often.'

She looked less unbelieving, but she sighed.

'Those places were a lot nearer then, than now,' she said. 'Oh, I don't mean the hills have moved, silly. Or the Lagan. I mean the city has spread out. You'd have a dreary trudge now, before you'd reach a green field, or a bit of river bank.'

Johnny's spirits were dampened. Then he caught sight of the tip of a crane over the roofs of the houses on the other side of the street. 'The docks haven't moved,' he said laughing. 'I read in a book that the gantries are the real cathedral spires of Belfast.' He saw he had impressed her. 'It's very nice down at the wharves. If the wind is blowing the right way you get a grand smell of the sea coming in off Strangford Lough.' But once more he was overcome by embarrassment. What if she thought he was suggesting she'd go down there with him? It was with a sweet shock he heard what she said next.

'If I was going down there, I'd have to tell my mother,' she said. 'Wait a sec, Johnny.'

When she half-skipped, half-danced away Johnny reached behind him and gave the doorknob a gentle pull, so the lock clicked. He wasn't going to risk facing his mother again. After all, he was doing what she wanted. Anyway, Eileen was coming back and he ran to meet her. As they walked up the street together, he tried to fit his stride to hers, but it wasn't easy because her high heels made her take short, uneven steps.

'Which way will we go?' she asked when they reached the top of the street. By common consent they headed in a direction that would avoid the centre of the city. Eileen was doing all the talking. As he listened to her, Johnny was so excited he couldn't hide it. Once, his ear caught a faint echo of the Orange drums in the distance and he looked uneasily at her, but she took no notice of the drums.

Soon the streets narrowed and the houses and shops got shoddier. At one corner their ears were assailed by a loud burst of drunken song coming through the louvred doors of a public house.

'What a way to spend the day.' Eileen said, but Johnny looked anxiously at the pub door thinking his father could be in there and could, at that moment, reel out into the street. It didn't seem honest to agree too wholeheartedly with Eileen.

'God help them,' he said, giving the excuse his mother always gave for his father's drinking. 'At least it's only themselves they're harming. They can't do too much damage even to themselves, with what little money they have in their pockets.'

'Money has nothing to do with it,' Eileen retorted. 'Protestants are all sober, the poor ones as well as the rich ones.' Johnny was startled by the way she rapped out the words.

'When did you ever see a poor Protestant?' he scoffed. 'If it comes to that, it's worth their while staying off the drink when they're holding down all the decent jobs in the city, with salaries that allow for putting something aside, for savings.'

'Those louts in that pub have their brains so rotted with booze they couldn't hold down a job, not if it was offered to them on a plate.'

'Nobody ever gave them anything on a plate. Or ever will, if you ask me,' he said, but she had confused him. Where did her sympathies lie?

Then, a few yards further on, they came to another pub, and once more song wafted out, although this time, the sound was not altogether unpleasant, as if the singers were younger and better able to hold their liquor. Eileen even smiled, and when they'd gone past, she began to hum the tune.

'Do you know that song?' she asked. Very softly she sang it, her voice sweet and true, but frail. Johnny was almost afraid to breathe in case its cadences be blown away. Then a line that he had heard with indifference scores of times caught his attention and unaccountably irritated him.

Albert Mooney says he loves her,
All the boys are crazy on her.

An odd notion came into his head and he frowned. She stopped singing.

'What's the matter?' she asked.

'Albert is a Protestant name,' he muttered.

'Oh, for God's sake. Do we have to drag religion into everything?'

He looked at her. 'You wouldn't go walking-out with a Protestant, would you?' he asked hoarsely.

Her contempt was blistering.

'I don't know any Protestants, Johnny Mack. I never spoke to one except maybe to an RUC man that once stopped me in broad daylight to ask if I had a lamp on my bicycle.'

That was the extent of his own acquaintance with them, but Johnny wasn't satisfied yet.

'Protestants are too bigoted to mix with us,' he said.

'That's beside the point,' she said coldly.

'They hate us,' he said doggedly.

'How do you know?' she rapped. 'How do we know what hate is if we don't have it in our own hearts?' She came to a stand again. 'Do you realize, Johnny Mack, that in other countries, civilized countries, people don't know, don't care, what religion you are? Do you think in England if a fellow liked a girl, he'd want to find out what church she belonged to before he'd speak to her? It's only in Belfast you get that muck.' She began to walk on. Now, above the rooftops, rising among the cranes and gantries, they could see the mast of a ship and gulls wheeling inward in slow circles, peering down hungrily at the litter in the gutters. Raucously then, right over their heads, a huge gull screamed and tried to wrest a scrap of refuse from the beak of another, both of them flopping about in the air.

'They'll fall on us,' Eileen screamed and caught his arm. 'Greedy things, thinking only of grub.'

Johnny had to laugh. 'Even nightingales forage for food,' he said.

She looked surprised.

'But nightingales aren't real, are they? You only get them in poetry.'

'Oh, they're real all right,' Johnny said, 'although you and I may never see one.'

To his delight she gave his arm a squeeze.

'Oh, Johnny, it's nice to be out with a fellow who reads books and can talk, talk the way you can about anything and everything, not just you and your own affairs.' She paused and a blush came into her cheeks. 'I may as well tell you, Johnny Mack, it was because I've seen you going into the library every week that I spoke to you today. I thought maybe you'd have more in your head than your brother, Sheamus, or my own gom of a brother.' Before he could answer, however, her face clouded. 'All the same I don't suppose you could have been brought up in the same house as Sheamus without flirting with some of his ideas?'

Flirting? To Johnny this was a word that had only one connotation. He was taken aback.

'Are we never going to come to those docks?' he exclaimed, to cover his feeling of awkwardness.

They were nearer to them than he thought. The next street was darkened by high warehouses and their way was frequently impeded by lorries and vans backing in and out of archways, loading and unloading. Now, along with the screams of gulls, there was the bawling of navvies and stevedores between whom dodged distraught clerks, with sheaves of lading bills flapping in draughts, from gateways and alleys. High in the sky, the long steel arms of cranes swung out, their giant-toothed buckets clanking angrily on their chains, as if ready to bite at random into anything that offered. From somewhere nearby, there stole a polluted smell of stagnant, land-locked water. This was not at all what Johnny had expected. Still, he hurried Eileen on.

Then, quite suddenly, at the end of the street, they flashed out on to the quayside and instantly everything changed. The breezes were now laden with a clean, briny smell, and seen against the blue sky, the arms of the cranes appeared frail as the webbed wings of a dragonfly. When a crane let down its bucket, it was seen that its prey was precisely designated, a crate or container upon which it laid hold, as delicately and deliberately as human fingers, to swing it aloft with a rhythm so true it dispelled fear.

Taking a deep breath of the sea air, Eileen sat down on a bollard, edging over to make room for Johnny. It amused him to see how neatly she fitted on less than half the bollard, while he could only hope to rest one hip on the half left for him. Even then, he had to make struts of his feet to prop himself up.

'It's nice here all right, isn't it?' Eileen said.

Johnny felt giddy with joy.

'You didn't really mean it when you said you'd leave here, if you got the chance, did you?' he asked.

'I did,' she said soberly. 'I'd go like a shot, wouldn't you?'

Johnny blinked. It had never entered his head that he would ever leave this city where he had been born.

'Well?'

'I don't know,' he said. Her question had unsettled him and he stared miserably out over the lough. Far out, angered by the offshore winds, the waves were choppy, but when they reached the harbour wall below him they nuzzled their snouts in tangles of black seaweed and shivered with delight. 'If it weren't for the curfew and the raids, Belfast wouldn't be such a bad place, would it?'

Eileen shook her head.

'I can't picture this place being any different from what

it's been all my life,' she said. She turned and faced him. 'How would you like to spend the whole of your days watching your words, with your mother waiting her chance to throw a cloth over your head like you'd cover a canary to stop it singing?' She was deadly earnest, but Johnny thought it was the funniest thing he'd heard in a long time.

'I wonder if Protestant mothers throw mufflers over their statues of King Billy every time a Protestant kid lets out a swear?' he said, laughing.

'Protestants don't curse or swear. Not before women anyway,' Eileen said primly.

'How do you know? You said you never spoke to one,' Johnny said. And at that she did laugh. 'Listen,' Johnny said. 'You know those Protestant houses with King Billy painted on the gable end, wouldn't it be great sport to sneak up some night and paint Billy green?'

Eileen giggled. 'Turn him into Saint Patrick?'

'Wait till I tell you something Sheamus and his pals did one night when they were kids. They painted the pillar box in our street green. The real joke of it was that next morning the RUC men didn't notice anything wrong and Sheamus saw them going off duty in the morning, swanking along pompous as ever, swinging their batons and . . .'

Eileen guessed what was coming and gave a little shriek. 'I know. Their backsides were all green.' Backside was not a word Johnny would have used in her presence, but inconsistency was what he had always expected from girls. He was getting happier and happier. 'That's the way to teach them, you know,' Eileen said. 'Make monkeys out of them. We'll never do it by sniping.'

'Ah, we'll never teach them anything, not by any means,'

Johnny said. A sudden gloom had come down on him again. 'Haven't we been trying for four hundred years?' He stooped and picked up a loose pebble from a heap of gravel at his feet. The feel of the stone in his fist worked upon him, and raising his arm, he flung it at a lamppost a few yards from where they sat. The stone pinged loudly against the metal reflector but did no harm.

'What made you do that? You could have broken that lamp,' Eileen said angrily.

'So what. I'd love to smash every lamp in Belfast,' Johnny said savagely. 'Often when I'm walking along the street, going about my own business, I can see the RUC staring at me like I was a mongrel that was going to lift his leg against one of their rotten lampposts.'

When Eileen said nothing he looked at her, and to his astonishment there were tears in her eyes.

'I'm not surprised you upset your mother,' she said. 'Such language. I thought you were different.'

Johnny wanted to cry out that, of course, he was different, but instead, he found himself reaching down for another stone, selecting it for its sharp edges, and this time, taking conscious aim, he fired it straight at the globe of the lamp. He missed again but only by accident, and an involuntary sigh of relief escaped him. He saw that Eileen knew he regretted his action.

'Come on, Johnny, we'd better be getting back.' She stood up. 'I told my mother I'd be home early.' She was now facing away from the lough, toward where between the warehouses, the hills of Divas could be seen, their green expanses darkened in places by the purple shadows of passing clouds.

What a place to put a cemetery,' she said inconsequentially and although it had never bothered him before,

Johnny looked with distaste at the vast cemetery that dominated Belfast. Then Eileen sighed. 'I suppose we ought not grudge the dead their last resting place up there in the peace and quiet,' she said sadly. 'Do you know what I think, Johnny? The only real patriotism in the world is the feeling people have for the sod. My mother told me once that the emigrants, before they went on to the ship, used to take up a fistful of earth and keep it all their lives, to be sprinkled on their coffins in the foreign land they were going to. The land was here before any of us, Catholics and Protestants.' Suddenly she faced back to the lough again, where a ship was heading out to sea. 'Oh, Johnny, supposing we were on that ship. Supposing we were leaving here forever.'

'Forever?' Johnny wondered was she joking.

'Well, perhaps not forever,' she said, 'but till all the hatred was burnt out of people's hearts.' Johnny looked so lost she laughed. 'Well maybe we might come back when there is no trace left of this wretched city, and when its dark, ugly churches of every creed and kind were heaps of stone with the green grass growing over them.'

Ah! Now Johnny understood. It was a fantasy.

'In three thousand years from now?' he cried. 'Oh, Eileen. We'd sail in like the Milesians.' She nodded, obviously unacquainted with ancient history but Johnny could see she was proud of his book learning.

'Come on, let's go home,' she said again. 'I didn't tell you, but when I went back for my coat and scarf, my mother said I could bring you home with me for tea if I wanted.'

Johnny's heart began to thump so violently he thought his ribs would crack.

'We can go back through Donnegal Square. It'll be

shorter, and the parade will be over by now.

Eileen hesitated.

'As long as we don't stop along the way,' she cautioned. 'Promise.'

Johnny promised. Together they stepped out happily, briskly, and although walking quickly, Johnny found it really hard to keep step with her tap-tappety heels.

'Why, in the name of God, do girls wear such crazy shoes?' he exclaimed.

'Every fellow asks that. Here, let me link you,' Eileen said. Immediately, one rhythm ran through them, and in no time, they were in the centre of the city.

The parade was over. Even the onlookers had gone, leaving the pavement scattered with cigarette butts and toffee wrappers. The few stragglers still in sight were heading homeward or making for their local pub. All the pubs in the city would soon be throbbing with song.

When they reached the residential area, Johnny and Eileen slowed down and began to stroll more leisurely. Johnny gave a sidelong look at her, but Eileen was staring in front of her. The quiet road had been empty when they first entered it, but now at the far end three youths were coming toward them. In this locality they would probably be Protestants, Johnny thought, but what did that matter? When he looked at Eileen, though, her face had gone white. He realized then that the advancing trio were walking abreast, arms linked, the full of the footpath. There would be no room for the two parties to pass. The three buckos were advancing upright and as purposeful as RUC men.

'Bloody bastards,' Johnny muttered.

'Johnny. Please.' Eileen tugged at his arm. 'Let's cross the street.'

'And let the likes of them push us into the gutter?'

'Oh, Johnny, what does it matter? Please, please,' she pleaded. She tried to unlink him, but he pressed her tighter to him. He could hear the feet of the oncoming youths marching in unison like the feet of soldiers, and like soldiers, they were spruced up and their boots were glossy with polish. Johnny was miserably aware of his ravelled gansey and tub-washed shirt, but above all, he was conscious of his cracked, unpolished boots. He raised his head and he simply couldn't believe his eyes: one of them, the one in the middle, was that bastard from the grammar school. As Eileen made another and almost frantic effort to drag herself free, he got confused. No. It was not the one in the middle that was his enemy. It was the one on the inside. Johnny's eyes slotted from face to face of the three, and it seemed to him that they all had the same face, the same hateful, sneering Protestant face. And it was at him they were sneering. For a moment, shame almost disarmed him. He nearly let Eileen pull him out of their way. But at that moment, the fellow on the outside doffed his cap to Eileen, and side-stepping like a dancer, fell back politely behind his companions, leaving place for her to pass. Eileen wrenched free from Johnny and went forward with lowered eyes.

Johnny felt his face go blood red. Now, with stinking Protestant politeness the bastard was waiting for him, too, to pass, but Johnny saw through him. Trying to show his superiority. That was it. He stood his ground. He would not pass. He looked quickly at the other two. But now he did not know which was the one he knew. Jer was right. All Protestants looked the same. And so he shot out his fist and smashed it into the nearest face. There was a thin sound like chicken bones breaking, and then Johnny broke into a run to catch up with Eileen.

But where was she? The street ahead was empty. Panic-stricken, he looked back. The fellow he'd hit was on the ground propped against the railings in a sitting position. The other two were ministering to him, a small pool of blood forming under their feet. Then he saw that Eileen was on the ground, too. Good God, what were they doing to her? He ran back madly, but when he pushed his way between the brutes, he saw Eileen was on her knees pressing a handkerchief to the face of the fellow he'd hit. Johnny gaped stupidly at her. After a moment or two one of the fellows helped her to her feet.

'You'd better go,' the youth said to her, and bending, he picked up her handkerchief that was soaked with blood. 'What will I do with this?' he asked. 'Will I have it washed and send it back to you?' Eileen said nothing, but Johnny snatched the handkerchief from him and stuffed it into his pocket.

'We have soap and water too,' he said hysterically, and he grabbed Eileen by the arm. But she broke away from him.

'Leave me alone,' she gulped. 'Go away.'

'What do you mean?' he demanded, ignoring the others. 'Your mother told you to bring me home for tea.'

She shook her head.

'It's too late, Johnny,' she said. Then when he went to protest, she held up her hand. 'I'm not talking about time by the clock,' she said. Johnny didn't know what she meant, but one of the other fellows sniggered, and to Johnny's relief, Eileen turned on him.

'What's so funny?' she demanded. She stared at the three youths in turn, including the fellow on the ground who was getting to his feet with a grin on his face. 'You were sneering at us, weren't you?' she said. She pointed to

Johnny. 'You were out to provoke him. You stupid fools. You think you're great, don't you? With your drums and sashes and your Union Jacks.' Then she swung towards Johnny. 'And you. You, with your Green, White and Gold. Soon there'll be only one flag in Belfast. Here, give me that,' she cried, and reaching forward, she pulled the blood-stained handkerchief out of Johnny's pocket and spiked it on the railings. 'There will be only one flag flying over this city soon,' she cried, and without another look at any of them, she walked away, going as steadily as was possible in her cheap papery shoes.

A Bevy of Aunts

My mother's sisters were raving beauties every one: Magdalene, Regina, Lally and Alice. My mother, whose name was Honor, dearly loved her sisters and talked endlessly about them. She talked about her brothers too, although I had ears only to hear about the aunts. For I was an only child who yearned for a sister and somehow guessed I would never be blessed with a sibling. Consequently at an early age I had decided to make do with one of the aunts as a surrogate sister. True, there was a certain disparity in age between me and them but that seemed of less consequence than the long remove at which we lived from each other. I lived in the small town in Massachusetts where I was born, and the aunts, with the exception of Magdalene, lived in Ireland, where they had been born. Up to the year I came into the world, Magdalene was the only aunt who had left Ireland, and before I was seven she had returned there. I was well acquainted with the appearance of my aunts, because of the truly monumental collection of photographs and other *memorabilia* of home that my mother had brought with her to America, which she kept under her bed in a cardboard dressbox that came originally from Moon's High Class Drapery in the city of Galway. I knew all there was to be known about them, how they dressed, how they wore their hair and what my mother called their endearing individual mannerisms.

The twelfth-century walled town in the west of Ireland where the family lived, was smaller than our town in Massachusetts, but it was so much more to my mother's liking that upon her arrival in her new home, she did not bother to unpack her trunk. 'Who?' she demanded of me when I was old enough to be her confidante, 'who would have appreciated its contents?' Certainly not the company my father had foolishly expected her to keep and still more foolishly expected her to enjoy as much as he himself had done before he married her.

Right from the start my mother had refused to accept my father's cronies. As for their wives, she declined to consider that their well-ordered homes with yeast bread rising in the oven and a cool beer always ready to hand in the ice box, ever constituted any excuse whatever for their not taking off their printed cotton aprons when they sat with their husbands of a summer evening on their front porches. By never going to their homes she felt free to discourage them from visiting ours. Those women had come to America as emigrants poor and uneducated and had gone into service with the family of the mill-owner by whom their husbands, like my father, were employed. With the training they got in that strict household, they were well equipped to run their own homes. It was only on exceedingly rare occasions they resorted to what they called home-help.

My mother's background was different. She came from a family that had given employment to girls like them. My grandmother had kept servants, who slept-in and wore starched white aprons in keeping with the fact that my grandfather's business, if no longer the most prosperous in the town, was conducted in a premises still the most imposing. It was a large, two-storied building of cut-granite, with the shop on the ground floor, and, except for the kitchen and one poky little parlour, the dwelling quarters were overhead, entered by a separate, private door. At home neither my mother nor my aunts had ever been asked to wet their fingers. There were always big strong country girls who carried the whole house on their shoulders and did everything for everyone. Inevitably those magnificently built and ambitious young women emigrated to America and when they did they were sorely missed by the whole family. My mother retained fond recollections of those amazons, and that the young women themselves reciprocated the affection of the household in which they had earned their passage money to the States was proved by gifts, often embarrassingly expensive, which they sent back to the family when they made good in the land of their adoption. There was, for instance, a canteen of solid silver cutlery from Tiffany's of New York with place-settings for twelve, of which one large table-spoon remains in my possession to this day, as testimony of their devotion. It was dug up in the manure heap of my grandmother's old garden after the property was sold and it was sent to me by the new owner who recognized it as belonging to my family by the monogram engraved on the handle. No doubt that tablespoon owed its survival to the carelessness of the inferior menials who, in later years, came to pass for servant girls. A lot more of it is probably lost forever under the ground.

As time went on, in order to meet the needs of a growing family, it was often found necessary to hire two or even three of these skittish young ones or 'baggages' as my grandmother called them. Indeed, in times of crisis there could be as many of them as there were daughters of the house, a number not outrageously excessive in view of their inefficiency and the enormous demands made upon them. They were on the go from morning to night, dashing up and down stairs, fetching and carrying, hauling heavy coal-hods, cleaning the globes of oil lamps, trimming wicks, heating curling tongs and racing across the cobbled yard every other minute to hang out corselets, buckram-lined bodices and other articles of apparel difficult to wash and still more difficult to dry. Delicate articles such as cambric camisoles with lace insets, crocheted collarettes and chamois gloves, my aunts had sense enough to launder themselves. But the task that took up most of the girls' time was the carrying of trays. How my mother used to laugh when she'd tell me of the collisions that often took place when the girls were running from room to room with those overloaded trays. I used to laugh too but I could not help thinking enviously of the fragments of broken china which, had I been there, I could have gathered up and added to my collection of *chaneys*, a word I learned from my mother's stories of her own childhood, and which I never afterwards heard in any part of the world not even when I myself eventually went to Ireland. Those *chaneys* would have been highly prized items in my collection. I felt sure there would have been fragments with an intact rosebud, a violet, a forget-me-not, or at the very least a bit with a gold-leaf rim because that china was Worcester, although this only came to light after my aunt Alice died when I was disposing of a pile of saucers that she used to put under clay pots of busy Lizzie which, as an old lady, she cultivated with mild enthusiasm.

Trays were the order of the day in my grandmother's home. After three unsuccessful, and seven successful conceptions, my grandmother had taken to having all her meals served in her bedroom. My grandfather soon took to having his meals brought to him in the shop, and ate standing at a high counting-house desk, where he strove to staunch leaks in ledgers that were filling up with debt as fast as an uncaulked boat with water. The uncles, Patrick and Vance, with the approval of my grandmother, whom they affectionately called Muggy, were daily gaining in authority over my grandfather, whom they called Foggy, and they were so intent on introducing innovations, intended – without success – to improve the business, they always ate at irregular hours in order to accommodate contractors, accountants and bank managers. More trays. As for the aunts, they stood behind the counter voluntarily in the evenings, trade being noticeably brisker when they did, and it was considered no more than natural that a tray of tea, a poached egg, or a bit of steamed fish might be fancied by one or other of them outside of proper meal hours.

But were there ever any proper meal hours? Was there ever a proper dining room, that is to say, a room that would have allowed a large family to sit down together at the same time? If such a room did once exist it must at some time have been incorporated into the shop. Or perhaps, when the aunts and uncles were young, they may have taken their meals in a small parlour downstairs, which had once been larger, a portion of it having clearly been partitioned off and a window blacked out to make a dark-room for my uncle Patrick who was an amateur photographer. In my mother's day, however, this parlour was held in contempt by all, being considered no better than a part of the shop, since it was used only as a waiting room for the wives of small farmers in from the country on Fair Days while their menfolk haggled outside in the streets with the cattle dealers. These womenfolk and their brood had to be plentifully supplied with trays of tea and biscuits, for the

same reason that their husbands' nags and jennets un-
hitched from their carts, and tied up in my grandfather's
yard, had to be provided with nosebags of oats, in the vain
hope that the hospitality thus dispensed would deter them
from taking their custom elsewhere, leaving the ledgers
swollen with their long-standing debts. 'The servant girls
were run off their feet catering for that tribe,' my mother
once said to my father.

'No wonder they emigrated,' my father said caustically.
'The wonder is that they ever got jobs in decent American
homes after the helter-skelter that went by the name of
work in your family.'

It was a wonder. It was also a fact. When, like their
inimitable predecessors, the scatter-brained 'baggages'
were in turn forced to emigrate, they too got good jobs.
Unfortunately for my mother two of them had found
employment in the same town to which my father brought
her as a bride. Worse still, they had married two of the
cronies.

My mother's homesickness, which had set in immediately upon her marriage, soon became chronic. She was
perpetually plaguing my father to bring her back to
Ireland. Be it said of him, that although he paid scant heed
to her pleas, I never heard him avert to her reason for
leaving home in the first place. She had done so at the
instigation of my grandmother, who had made her see that
it was her duty as the eldest of the family to get out and
make way for her younger sisters. She thereupon accepted
a proposal by post from my father with whom she was
barely acquainted, having only known him for a few days
when he was on his first trip home after twenty years, and
spending money like a lord.

Perhaps my mother did not know how well entitled her

mature suitor was to this splurge, since he had already
invested the best part of his lifetime's savings in the Boston
State Street Trust Company. And, had she known, would
she have been impressed? She had never been inculcated
with the virtue of thrift. In her book it was equated with
tight-fistedness.

After supper on Saturday nights when my father would
put his hand in his pocket and produce a wad of dollar bills
to count out her housekeeping money, she always took that
moment to stand up from the table and clear away the
dishes, leaving the dollars disregarded among the crumbs.

My mother had no gift for bringing out my father's
innate generosity, a gift I apparently had in aggravating
abundance. Nickles, not dollars, was the currency in which
he and I dealt, but these he rained down on me so hard and
fast that when he died, and I was already married and had
three girls of my own, I was truly surprised to find he had
left me a nice-sized legacy.

In spite of their differences, my parents' marriage could
not be said to have been a conspicuous failure. They made
the best of a bad job. My father sustained himself by going
on an occasional batter with the cronies, but more so by
daily gratitude to God for having given him a child at a late
age. My mother sustained herself by pride in having put
filial duty before all else, and by a belief that she had set an
example to her sisters, although, in the end only one of
them came anywhere near to following her lead, and that
one got even less reward for her pains than my mother.

Looking back, it seems to me now that although both
my parents must have been aware that they had not had a
large measure of happiness, they must nevertheless have
been blinded to the full extent of their lack of it. They
customarily made remarks in each other's hearing, which,

if offence was intended, was not taken. I often heard my mother claim, in my father's hearing, that she had taken an instant dislike to him the first time she saw him. Yet he seemed to regard this a tribute. Perhaps he thought it made his subsequent conquest of her the more impressive. Or perhaps he had led himself to believe that an initial display of dislike on the part of a woman was coquetry, and as good a basis for marriage as the love at first sight on which his choice of her had been founded. He never made a secret of the impact her beauty had had upon him, nor of the fact that he had set his cap at her from the start.

'She was a stunner,' he said time and again, stoutly maintaining that if he had to live his life over, he would go all out to get her, as he had done the first time. 'No matter what!' he'd add. Happening to make this boast in the company of the cronies one Sunday after mass, when we ran into them in the church grounds, I saw them look down at their boots to hide their grins. Yet my mother accepted the compliment, and the implications of his rider to it passed over her head.

The cronies were well aware of my mother's homesickness and they were sorely troubled in case it would infect my father. They repeatedly urged him to take a strong line and put a stop to her nonsense. And so, it never occurred to me that, except for Magdalene whom I had already met, I might some time see my aunts in the flesh.

Then one day when my mother had gone to Boston for the day and the cronies had ventured in for a few hours before her train was due back, my father made an extraordinary pronouncement. Sitting happily in his shirt-sleeves he began to talk about Ireland. 'Honor will never get me to go back there again on a visit, but it's God's own country and when I go back I'll go for good. When I've made enough money I'll pack up, lock, stock and barrel, and it's there I'll end my days.'

I could scarcely believe my ears and from that day on I paid fanatical attention to every word about her old home that fell from my mother's lips. Soon I could have made my way blindfold around the whole place. I could have run out across the cobbled yard and found my way easily between the ramification of sheds and storehouses to the corroded iron-gate that led into the garden, knowing it would be wild and overgrown, having implicitly believed my mother's proud assertion that a garden *so* large, simply *had* to become neglected. There was of course a path kept open in it to get to the clothes line. And every summer the grass was scythed under an old apple tree where my grandmother took tea if there came a really fine day.

On such a day my uncle Patrick would bring out his camera and tripod to take shots of the family grouped around a wicker tea table, making the two youngest members, Vance and Alice, strew themselves on the grass, holding their delicate cups in their hands like chalices. If some member of the family was by chance absent, a sticky-back of the missing one was pasted in the corner of the photograph. Sadly, no one ever took note of the fact that Patrick could not include himself in the groups and so there were few likenesses of him in existence, a circumstance which was to be a lasting sorrow to my mother in after years. She did not have a single picture of Patrick, not even in a special album with blue linen covers which was devoted to formal studio portraits taken by a professional photographer in Galway, because these were mainly portraits of the aunts.

Surprisingly there were no portraits of my mother. She explained this omission by confessing that she had never

been content with any likenesses ever attempted of her. She
had destroyed them all. A few informal snapshots of her
that did survive seemed to prove her right about her
discontent, although it must have predated the click of the
camera. Certainly no cameraman had elicited from her the
smiles they had coaxed from her sisters, smiles that were
facsimiles of those I had seen on postcard pictures of Zena
Dare and Lily Langtry, which were also preserved in that
dress box along with programmes from shows in which
they had starred on the stage of the Tivoli Theatre in
Dublin to which Patrick had on occasion taken my mother.
Patrick was her eldest brother and her favourite apart from
Vance, the youngest of the family, whom, however, she
loved in a maternal way.

In addition to those outdoor photographs, Patrick had
also experimented with a few indoor shots. There was one I
particularly liked. It had been taken in the big, upstairs
drawing-room. Patrick must have been very proud of it
because he had it enlarged and, according to my mother,
beautifully framed for her as a going-away present.
Unfortunately, she had to take it out of the frame to bring it
to America. In it Magdalene and Lally were standing to one
side of the marble fireplace, their arms entwined, and
Regina, with a rose in her hair, was seated on the piano-
stool as if she had just swivelled around to say a word to
Alice who was about to turn a page of the music.

All of them were wearing the most bewitching dresses,
the skirts had the amplitude of full blown roses while the
bodices were as tight as unopened rose-buds, and neck-
bands, wristbands, hems and belts were embellished either
with the finest of hand tucks, with beading, passmenterie
or, at the very least, with intricately worked silk braiding.
These embellishments – my mother explained – were to

add touches of colour, vermeil or coral or old rose, because as I had already been given to understand, the aunts in general favoured dresses in soft shades, oyster, pearl or dove which would not compete unfairly with their own colouring, since, with the exception of Alice, they all had light brown, almost fair, hair.

Alice was dark and for a long time I used to think her dresses were black until my misconception came to light in a stray remark. My mother was scandalized.

'Black? What *are* you talking about? Only widows wore black in our day. That's *brown*. Alice always wore brown. She chose the most enchanting shades, tobacco, cinnamon or chestnut. And she always wore a taffeta bow to match on her hair.'

'To match her dresses?' I asked because I had a boxful of bows to match my dresses. Tied to the ends of my pigtails they made the pigtails less hateful. But I was wrong.

'No, to match her hair.'

How I marvelled at all this finery, but I marvelled too at the magnificence of the drawing-room in which the photographs had been taken and which my mother had always told me was unusually spacious for a business house in a small Irish town, but I could see it would want to have been roomy to accommodate the vast collection of furniture, ornaments and bric-à-brac with which my grandmother had filled it, having acquired everything cheaply at auctions throughout the years, as the big houses of the landed gentry went down one by one under the auctioneer's hammer. Indefatigably for a woman of delicate health she had gone to those auctions and collected item after item until her drawing-room was crammed to capacity with encoignures, consoles, teapoys, an ottoman, a davenport, a love seat and, as its crowning glory, a grand piano, which, for all its size, could have passed almost unremarked in the magnificent clutter of its surroundings.

To this day it is a mystery to me how a simple townswoman, born in a remote part of an impoverished region, orphaned at thirteen and married at sixteen to one of her own shop boys, could have been endowed with so great a gift for discerning the beauty of the things she amassed. One can only suppose that being of a practical nature, she could tell a well-made article from gimcrack and seized bargains when she chanced upon them.

It is to be hoped that in her youth she was happy in the possession of her treasures before graver concerns eventually made her indifferent to their fate, which was to be thrown out into sheds and outhouses where most of them would be reduced in no time to matchwood.

In my mother's heyday when she left for America that drawing-room was the pride and glory of the whole family.

To return to the aunts, however, for whom the drawing-room was only a backdrop, I had still to make up my mind on which aunt was to be my make-believe sister.

As the youngest, Alice ought to have been my most obvious choice but I truly believe it was hearing about the bow on her hair that made me finally pick her. The fact that she was wearing a bow at all made her seem nearer in age to me although, oddly enough I never could see the bow in the photographs. I supposed it to be fastened on the nape of her neck, and to hang down her back like a sash. But it counted a lot that her hair was not piled up in a bun on the top of her head like my mother's and Magdalene's and Lally's. Alice's hair hung loose to her shoulders. It was straight, of course, not curly like her sisters, but then, mine was straight too. And to be candid I was secretly pleased that her hair was shorter than mine, very much shorter, only shoulder length, whereas mine if it was released from the hideous braids in which it was imprisoned, would have reached my waist. I could have sat on it. I really could. This seemed to give me a certain equality with Alice because there was no doubt that the way she wore her hair was very striking. It spread out either side of her face, stiffly, and shapely and as widely as the wing-span of a bird on the hover.

Finally I made up my mind to have Alice as my sister. Honesty, however, compels me to admit that I had for a long period been inclined to choose Regina. After all she was only a year older than Alice, and her hair, too, was not bundled up in a bun like her older sisters. It was dressed in a special style, of which I was already enamoured. Regina's hair was the nearest to golden of all the aunts, and it too was braided, but when she was still very young she was allowed to wear her braids wound around her temples in a kind of a crown. And, if those golden braids were let out, I am sure that she, too, like me could have sat on her thick tresses.

Unfortunately, I suffered a bitter humiliation on account of Regina's hair and that was what put Alice on top of my list.

One day poring over the box of photographs, it had occurred to me that perhaps I, too, could wear my braids in a wreath across my forehead. Encouraged by the knowledge that two of my schoolmates wore their hair in that fashion, although admittedly one was Swiss and the other was German, I broached my plan to my mother. I got short shrift.

'Regina was allowed to wear her hair like that because of her name,' she said. Knowing that Regina's pet name was Queenie, I understood and accepted that I had no such rights, but I could see my father had taken umbrage on my behalf.

'What do you mean by that,' he enquired.

Wincing at his ignorance of Latin, my mother did not deign to reply, but I felt we had not heard the end of the matter.

My father was inordinately proud of my hair. It was as black as pitch, like his own had been when he was young, as straight as a ramrod, and as thick as thatch. And so one afternoon when I was with him in the livery stables at the mill, where he was overseeing the grooming of the horses that were to draw the mill float in the Labour Day Parade, supervizing the combing of their manes and the plaiting of their tails, he remarked to me and to all and sundry, that there would not be a single horse in the whole parade that would have a mane or a tail to compare with my shiny braids. And when we got home he whispered to me that I ought to go upstairs and borrow a few of my mother's tortoiseshell hairpins and try out my hair in the coil I fancied.

Alas, I had no sooner done so, than I learned from the mirror, the reasons for my mother's disapproval. Two ropes of black, black hair, as coarse as hemp, wound around my head was a sorry sight. And for the first time I began to think about family likenesses, and taking out the hairpins I ran downstairs. 'Oh Mother, isn't it a pity my grandmother didn't have me, then I might be a beauty like you and my aunts.'

My mother looked at me in dismay. 'Why do you say that? Don't you like having me for a mother?'

'Oh I do. I do. but I'd still have you because then you'd be my sister.'

My mother's dismay was dispelled and she laughed, but after a moment a bemused look came on her face. 'Where would your father have fitted into that scheme of things?' she asked, almost to herself.

I'd forgotten about my father, but at the thought that I might have had any other father in the whole world, I burst into tears.

'Don't worry,' my mother said, 'It's too late in the day to alter matters now.' And she went on with whatever she was doing.

About this time a series of events occurred in my mother's family which of themselves narrowed my options down to Alice. Magdalene had, from the start, been excluded because as I've said I had already met her and although she was young and beautiful she seemed too motherly for a sister.

Magdalene was the second eldest of the aunts, next after my mother. And she was next to leave home, because when my mother realized that I was on the way her homesickness flared to such dangerous proportions that my father, in defiance of the cronies, made enquiries in the shipping office of the Cunard White Star office about a passage to Ireland for her. According to the shipping office it was not advisable for her to travel in her condition. By an odd chance at exactly that same time, back in Ireland my grandmother discovered that an assistant in another and smaller shop than my grandfather's had had the audacity to pay court to Magdalene, who in her simplicity did not see the inappropriateness of his suit.

What better under such circumstances than to give Magdalene time to reconsider things? And where better to do so than in America in the company of her older sister, Honor, to whom she could meanwhile be a comfort at the time of the accouchement?

Such comfort as Magdalene gave my mother at that delicate time has gone unrecorded, but it evidently did little to alter her feelings for the sweetheart she had left behind, because years afterwards she married him when death deprived him of the wife with whom he had consoled himself for loss of her, and who had given him a houseful of sons.

Magdalene had the most charm, and was the most universally loved of the aunts. She had more beaux than had all her sisters put together. Admirers flocked as thickly around her in America as they had in Ireland. My father had his hands full fending off – at her request – eligibles and ineligibles alike. On both she had looked askance.

Upon her arrival in America it was understood by Magdalene, as well as by my parents, that she would only be staying a few months, but the War broke out and held her captive there for five years. My father decided she must take a job. With her looks and good manners, he had no difficulty in getting her a position in the office of the mill. She was so overjoyed, so happy in the job that she was astonished to hear the good salary she was to be paid. She was to be still more astonished at the end of her first week's work, when she proudly emptied out her pay-packet on our kitchen table to find my father scoop up all but a few dollars, and announce that he was going to invest the rest for her. This he did, with the luck that always attended him in such matters. Her gilt-edged stocks rose so phenomenally that in no time at all she was a comparatively wealthy woman. The first thing she did was buy a big car. And when she went back home she brought the car with her. She must have been one of the first women in Ireland to drive a car of its size. This gave her a status accorded only to married women in those days.

We missed her dreadfully when she left us, but back in Ireland she cut a great dash with her American money, her American ways and above all with her big American car.

The car was always packed with youngsters because she loved children, and children loved her. She acted on them like a magnet. Every child in the town called her Aunt Magdalene. The smaller ones believed she was their aunt by blood. The older ones, who knew better, wished it were true.

By a cruel irony the only young people who did not take to her were her stepchildren. From the outset of her marriage to their elderly father, they rejected her every advance. This went a long way towards poisoning her joy in a marriage which, to tell the truth, had appeared more romantic in her eyes than it had in the eyes of others.

When, inevitably and quite naturally, her stepsons married and left home, Magdalene persuaded herself she had driven them out. In her unceasing struggle for their love, although she died unvictorious, there shone about her in her declining years the luminosity that alone can eclipse the glare of victory, the light of valiance in the face of defeat.

I went to see her in hospital when she was dying, and I deliberately brought my second husband with me because ours too was a late marriage. She was very weak but she made the nurses prop her up on pillows the better to look at him. 'I'm glad to see you are a handsome man,' she whispered.

'You're easy on the eyes yourself,' he said. Whereupon she gave him the smile with which she had charmed so many men, women and children, but not, to her sorrow, those whom she wanted most in this world to please.

Shortly after Magdalene had returned to Ireland, news came from there that nearly broke my mother's heart. Her brother Patrick died in the influenza epidemic that swept across Europe in the wake of the war, but conditions were still similar to those of wartime, and although in the course of the previous four years we had been hearing almost daily of young men we knew blown to bits in Flanders, the Somme or the Marne, that news travelled fast in military despatches, whereas the news of civilian deaths came slowly. Patrick was a month in his grave before my mother heard about it. That made it so much harder on her that thereafter she could never feel sure but that at any moment of the day or night some other member of her family might be on the point of expiring. Consequently, she hourly punctuated our conversation with a pious ejaculation in which I was called upon to join. *Lord have mercy on the dying and the dead.* This she and I would intone at times and in places so unsuitable, in the street, in a shop or on a trolley car, that people stared at us in amazement. Luckily they must have told themselves that my mother was suffering a carry-over of war neurosis, or that there was probably some poor wounded soldier, a young husband perhaps, on his way home from France aboard one of the hospital ships in which so many never made it alive to port.

In the months that followed the news of Patrick's death my mother found life in America more unbearable than ever. One day, however, news of another kind found its way to us. It too came circumlocutiously in a rumour my father picked up at the mill from the cronies. He came in the door as pleased as Punch to tell us. 'You won't believe what I heard today! Regina is married.'

My mother put her hand to her heart. 'How could you blurt out a thing like that? Don't you know that good news can be as much of a shock as bad?'

My father was greatly taken aback. Clearly his tidings had not been received in the way he expected. 'If you think that news is good news, I may as well tell you she eloped.'

Opprobrium now blazed openly in his eyes. 'They say she ran off with an RIC man,' he shouted. But again he was cheated by mother's reaction.

'I know him,' she said rapturously. 'A fine man! he always had his eye on Regina. She fancied *him* too, no matter how much she denied it, we knew, we knew. And see how right we were!'

My father was now completely baffled although he ought to have known better than to have taken political opinions at secondhand, because he himself was in no way politically minded.

Neither of my parents held strong views on Irish nationalism, my father by reason of having grown up in a part of the land so desolate, boggy, barren and unpeopled he did not find out until he got to Boston that the Royal Irish Constabulary stalked other prey than young scholars playing truant in the demesnes of the landed gentry, tickling trout in their rivers, and catapulting at pheasants in their woods – my mother by reason of the family's shop being opposite the RIC barracks where the Constabulary were not only regular customers, but among the few who paid cash, and paid on the nail.

'Well? I hope she'll be happy anyway.' My father gave in gracefully enough.

'She will,' my mother said, with confidence. 'Regina has got a good man.' Her words were nearer the mark than she knew. Regina's husband was truly good. When he was a boy it is likely that he too did not know much of what was going on outside the lonely farm in Mayo where he was raised. I doubt if he knew the difference between the Union Jack and the rebel flag, although he was not long in the Constabulary until he found out. Nor was he long about acting on his newly acquired knowledge. It was said of him that at risk to his own life he saved the life of many a man in green. So, when his country finally got its freedom, and the RIC was disbanded, his certificate of honourable discharge from the service of His Majesty the King of England meant less under the new conditions in Ireland than did the respect and esteem in which he was held by his fellow countrymen. Aided by them, he quickly found a job in private life, which spoke volumes for the esteem in which he was held. It is chastening to think that he was probably the nearest my mother's family ever came to possessing a patriot.

Regina certainly married the right man. She never lost sight of that fact either. She gave him so many children she used to laugh shamefacedly when asked their number. Not that she blushed at love's device, but merely at the prodigality of its outcome. She was the only one of the aunts whose marriage was enduringly happy. Her love for her husband outlived him, and it sustained her so well in the long years of her widowhood that when she grew old she became obese, a rare feat for a woman who had had to rear a large houseful of children single-handed. When I first met her she was an old woman, but she was always laughing, often so convulsively that her whole body shook and it was impossible not to laugh with her. Her home was the happiest in Galway city to which she moved when her children were growing up. Theirs was a good sized house but the bedrooms were used only for sleeping, the sitting-room for giving the piano lessons by which she eked out a small pension, and God alone knows what use was made of the dining-room, until she became so heavy she could not climb the stairs when it came into use as a bedroom for her. The kitchen was the core of that house. Into it all the family managed to squeeze themselves every evening along with the multitude of their friends whom she, as much as the young people, attracted to the house.

But to go back to the days when Regina was young and we first heard of her elopement. In the very same year we received almost identical news of Lally. She too had run off to Dublin and got married. This time the news arrived directly in a letter from Alice, so my mother was the one to announce it. Lally too had eloped. My mother was once again overjoyed at the news. 'I'm not in the least surprised,' she said. 'Robert was madly in love with Lally, even when they were school children.'

I shared my mother's bliss. By then I thought elopement was the peak of romantic love. I did not know that there were homes where the back door was the sole door open to hot-blooded young lovers.

My father was noticeably less than blissful. 'I met him, didn't I?' he asked. 'A sickly little fellow? A cripple?'

'Only a slight limp. Like Lord Byron,' my mother said indignantly.

My father, of course, had never heard of Byron, but regardless of this my mother warbled on. 'Robert was always reading poetry. He used to read it to Lally on summer evenings sitting on the rampart wall. You have no idea how good looking he was. He had a head of black curls and –' Here she gave a little cry. 'Lord Byron had curly hair too – isn't that remarkable.'

She had gone too far. My father's small store of patience had run out. 'If he's the young fellow I met, he didn't look like a fellow who would ever lay hands on much money.'

My mother came down from the clouds. 'Money isn't everything in this world,' she said coldly.

'Is that so?' My father raised his eyebrows. 'Well, you can't deny it's worth a bit more in this world than it will be in the next.' But he looked more sad than angry. Lally was easily the most beautiful of the aunts, and doubtless it distressed him to think that hardship might diminish her beauty. 'Poor Lally,' he murmured.

As things turned out, Lally and her young husband were not long in Dublin until she was so bedraggled her family were ashamed if any of the townspeople, up in the city for a few days' shopping, ran into her in the street. Her neighbours loved and respected her. Perhaps they assessed her shabby apparel as they would assess the habit of a nun, and saw it as an outer manifestation of an inner state. For so it was. Life had begun to confuse her. Yet her fleshly beauty seemed indestructible. To the last, her form was shapely as a girl's, her movements free and swift. And her skin took the weather like a bird takes it on its plumage. Although her hair got dry and wild, it never seemed greyer than if she'd been dusting out a cupboard or sweeping the yard. And her eyes, that were once blue as a sky in summer, became bluer than ever when the storm clouds broke. Then, they blazed with the fierce blue flash of lightning tearing its way through a night sky. Of all the aunts I loved her best.

By the time I eventually met Lally, her husband was an invalid, and she was sorely harassed by her efforts to support him and his children. If her clothes were scruffy, her house was a shambles. Yet there was not a lazy bone in her body. It was her untameable spirit that wreaked havoc around her. Whenever she took the notion of putting her house to rights, she went to work with the force of a cyclone and laid it more waste than before. Her energy was phenomenal. At the end of a hard day she had hoarded up enough strength to use the last of the light to grub around in her narrow garden that lay between the gardens of the houses to either side, but whereas theirs were one and all trodden bare as a hen-run, hers, winter and summer, was like a corner of a public park. In winter a profusion of evergreens billowed over her fences, and formed dark groves where early snowdrops came out with the thrilling suddenness of the first stars of evening. And in summer flowering climbers entwined in this greenery, burgeoned into blossom. In that sooty city soil she could coax any plant, however tender, to grow and luxuriate. You'd be tempted to think she could have reaped a harvest of emeralds and sapphires, if she had had a few chippings to use for seed.

Was she happy? Who knows? In the end, past, present and future became inextricable in her mind, all part of the enigma life finally became for her.

One evening in late spring, when her own spring time was long past, I called at her house, and not finding her inside went out to the garden where I came upon her standing motionless under a quivering poplar. The tree was rooted in the garden next door but through the years it had contrived to stretch its leafy branches over the fence and sing its songs for her ears. I was afraid I would startle her until when she turned I saw she had forgotten the earth on which she stood.

In the vanishing light of that evening I was reminded of my childish yearning for a sister, a yearning of which I was rid long before my parents compounded their differences and decided to settle in the land of their birth. Then only one of the aunts remained unmarried, Alice. She and Vance still remained with Muggy in the old home, but I had vaguely expected I was going to step back into the world of those old photographs on which I had founded the obstinate dreams of an only child.

★　　　★　　　★

It was autumn when my mother and I set sail from Boston on the SS Winefredian, my father having despatched us ahead to buy a home in Dublin while he remained behind to dispose of our effects. The custody of the Irish ports had not yet been given back by the British to the new Republic of Ireland, so we could not land at Cobh. We had to go on to Liverpool and from there come back across the Irish Sea and travel the length of Ireland by rail.

We took a late train and it was night when it slowed down to enter the dimly lit station where we were the only passengers to descend. I thought we had slipped into a siding, until the carriage windows threw their light on the platform and there was my uncle Vance, his face beaming all over with smiles. The train hadn't altogether stopped when he ran alongside our carriage and, wrenching open the door, jumped in and almost bowled us over with his welcome.

'Vance, you reckless fellow,' my mother chided him at the same time that she hugged and kissed him. 'How tall you've grown! I hardly recognized you. You were only a little chap in short pants when I went away.'

'Time, alas, does not stand still Honor,' he said sadly, and I suddenly remembered my mother once telling me that he was the one who missed her most when she went away because their mother being delicate it was she who had really mothered him. In her box of mementoes there was a faded page of a child's copy-book of his, in which he had written a poem and given to her to take with her to America.

Of all the people I love best
I love the mother of the nest

I thought it was written about my grandmother until I'd

seen tears in my mother's eyes and realized it was about her he had written it. I was wondering if she remembered that poem, when the guard blew his whistle and threw them both into a state. 'This train does not stand still either. The stop here is only four minutes,' Vance said and he began in a frenzy to get our suitcases out on the platform and to help us down after them.

'Oh mind my flowers,' my mother said as she herself took down the bunch of carnations which, it seemed to me, she had cherished inordinately throughout our long journey since they had been given to her on the eve of our departure by one of the despised cronies. She had safeguarded them all the way across the Atlantic, keeping them in the handbasin in our cabin, and, to the manifest contempt of our stewardess who was ruthlessly disposing of other flowers, even orchids that had been left behind by our fellow passengers, she had carried them ashore at Liverpool, and from there across the choppy Irish Sea, wrapping them in wet newspaper when we got to Dublin in preparation for five hours in a hot and stuffy railway carriage. 'They're as fresh as when we started,' she said proudly and indeed they had not lost a single petal although from being bright pink they had acquired a peculiar reddish tinge.

We had scarcely got ourselves and our belongings out on to the platform when the train began to make a shunting noise preparatory to pulling out.

'Vance! Vance. Are you sure we left nothing behind? Did you look on the rack? On the seats? Did you try *under* the seats?' Then she gave a little shriek 'My trunk! It's in the guard's van,' she cried. Vance only laughed and pointed to an old man coming towards us with our trunk loaded up on a wooden handcart with noisy, iron-shod wheels. He took

off his cap to my mother and began to pile our cases on top
of the trunk. My mother gave a great sigh of relief and let
herself be persuaded to place the carnations on top of the
lot. When the cart was trundled away she stopped fussing
and looked around her. Next minute she was ready to start
more commotion. '*Alice*?' she said 'Where is Alice? Why
isn't she here to meet me?' But the train that had begun to
move was now picking up speed and as the lights of its
carriages passed over us, they seemed to seek out our faces
like searchlights and Alice was temporarily forgotten as my
mother scrutinized Vance. 'I can't get over how tall you
are,' she said. 'And thin.' She frowned 'Too thin. You're a
regular beanstalk. What's all this Alice has been telling me
in her letters about you turning into a real lady-killer,
gallivanting off every weekend to Lisdoonvarna or
Lahinch? I hope that does not mean cheap hotels with poor
food and damp bedding?'

'Not any more,' Vance said. 'That was in my salad days.
Since Foggy died I've had my work cut out keeping the
business together. Poor Foggy's methods were a long way
behind the times. Patrick had already made a few changes
before his death but when I had to run the place single-
handed I had to be more drastic if I was to keep us afloat.'

As my mother was listening she began to look worried,
but Vance appeared quite happy. 'I seldom go away
anywhere now. You see, Alice has blossomed out and she
and her friends provide plenty of distraction here at home.
They have what they call social evenings which means
hammering on the piano and singing and all kinds of
codology. They've practically turned the house into a
music hall.'

'Not *our* house,' my mother sounded incredulous, 'What
about Muggy? The least noise used to upset her after she
went to bed.'

But now the train had plunged into a tunnel at the end of the platform, taking its lights with it and leaving us submerged in the dim and sickly light of a fly-blown lantern hanging from a nail outside an empty waiting room. 'Oh how different this is from the day I left,' my mother exclaimed. 'I'll never forget the excitement of that day. So many people came to see me off. The platform was thronged, simply thronged, with well-wishers all wanting to bid me God speed. It was daytime of course and that made a difference. Poor Patrick was alive then too.'

'And Foggy,' I piped up.

'Ah poor Foggy. He was too good for this world,' my mother said.

'And too soft,' said Vance.

My mother put her hand to her forehead. Something had escaped her mind. 'Did Foggy come to the train with us that day? I can't for the life of me remember. Probably not. He hated leaving the shop without one of the family in attendance. He was so conscientious. It was pathetic at times.'

'Specially towards the end,' Vance agreed. 'But why are we standing here in the cold? Let's get going.'

Outside the station we found ourselves in pitch darkness. 'Oh dear,' my mother was taken by surprise, 'I'd forgotten how far the station was from the town. You don't mean to say you haven't yet got town lighting? In America the smallest village, a mere halt, has electricity.'

'Well, you're not in America now, Honor,' Vance said quietly.

'That's obvious,' my mother replied but she squeezed his arm affectionately. 'I'm not complaining, it's just hard to believe I'm home again after all I've gone through. Let's hurry.'

Then, three abreast with me between them we started off

down the middle of a street as dark as a country road in Massachusetts. To one side of us there were trees but the real darkness came from the highest wall I ever saw in my life, a wall as high as a house, and covered all the way up with ivy. Looking at it I stumbled once or twice.

'Here, let me give the child a piggy-back.' Vance picked me up and setting me astride his shoulders he started to jog-trot ahead of my mother.

'Stop that tomfoolery, Vance, the child is well able to walk,' my mother said. I thought he would not pay any heed to her but he'd begun to breathe very heavily and he did put me down. Anyway we had left the wall behind and it was not so dark. The trees too were thinning out and surprisingly the sky was brimming with stars. My mother stopped for a minute and gave a brief glance back over her shoulder. 'I can't believe the old rampart wall is still standing,' she said and she turned to me, 'I told you about the ramparts, didn't I?'

I was too indignant to answer. Of course I knew all about that ancient wall that ran almost all the way round the town, and was so wide two people could walk side by side along the top. Wasn't my mother always talking about the way she and the aunts used to walk along it to take the air on summer evenings, encountering friends in pursuit of the same ends? She told me what a tricky business it was sometimes for couples to get past each other without going in single file. But that was part of the fun. Chivalry now and then demanded that a young man jump down into the dried-up moat on the outside which gave rise to a lot of jollity, but I was assured that it would not have been considered the least bit funny if anyone fell down on the inside, which was a wilderness of nettles and briars. 'Is the place still as overgrown and neglected as ever, Vance?' she asked, looking back again.

'Worse if anything. It's really an unwholesome place now. It's a danger to public health. It has become a dumping ground, with litter of all kinds thrown over the wall. I heard recently that it's in there the local butchers jettison their offal and poultry cleanings.'

I listened in surprise. I thought I knew all about the ramparts, but until then I thought the word rampart designated only the wall and not the land *inside* it. Being at all times as unburdened as my mother had always been by any great weight of history, I did not know that what she and her family and friends considered a town, had once been a royal city, and that within its enclosure, their outlines blurred by ivy, were the remains of a king's castle and the topless ruin of a famous priory. Years later when I was a student in Dublin, it crossed my mind that for all their disregard of past history, there must still have been a vague ancestral memory of it buried deep in the minds of the townspeople because nothing else could account for their sense of superiority over those who lived outside the town boundaries, although many of them were comfortable farmers with well stocked acres of land.

That night walking from the station, however, I was sure my mother and Vance were right to deplore the condition of the place, and its gross misuse.

'It's a shame, a real shame to think of that valuable land going to waste. In America land like that would be considered a prime building site, priceless real estate.'

Vance nodded in gloomy agreement. 'It would be regarded as priceless here too, and properly utilized long ago, if it were not for a number of cranks from Dublin who come down here off and on ranting and talking rot about our wonderful national heritage and our duty to preserve the irreplaceable glories that remain to us of what they call our "unique legacy".'

'But surely nobody listens to them?' My mother found it hard to believe such a thing was possible. 'We have crackpots like that in America too, people not smart enough to make money who want to be thought smarter than those who do. We just ignore them. Why can't you do the same? After all no one paid any heed to poor Foggy and *he* used to go around mumbling something of that nature, if I recall correctly. He was a dear old silly-billy wasn't he? Do you know I sometimes think I take after him. I'm a real silly-billy myself at times. You will hardly believe it but when our train was pulling into the station tonight I forgot for a second that it was not long ago and I really and truly expected – well let's say I half expected – to find the whole family on the platform to welcome me. Not only Foggy and Patrick but all the girls as well, Magdalene, Regina, Lally and – ' She stopped here abruptly, 'You did't explain why Alice didn't come to the train.'

When Vance whispered the explanation for her absence, it was fortunate that my mother's surprise led her to voice such loud and indiscreet questions that it became immediately apparent to me why Alice had not come.

'Packing? To go to stay with Regina? Regina can't be "on the way" again? So soon? And why does Alice have to go *tomorrow*? Are there complications expected? And for how long is she going?'

This torrent of questions was satisfied by one, single answer from Vance. 'I don't know anything about it,' he said. 'But when she and Muggy heard you were coming they decided it would give Alice the chance of a little holiday. She's been very tied down here for the past few years since all the others left.'

My mother, who had got a shock, rallied quickly. 'Oh I wouldn't want her to cut short her stay on my account. For that matter I'll be only too glad to have Muggy all to myself. I'll have so much to tell her! Although I must say I can't see why Alice has to go tomorrow, my very first day home.'

'But we understood you were only going to be here a very short time, that your husband sent you ahead of him to buy a house in Dublin.'

'That's right, but there's no hurry about it. Goodness knows I've been away long enough, I deserve a little vacation myself.

'That's true,' Vance said, but I didn't think he sounded too enthusiastic. 'I see no reason why you shouldn't enjoy your stay, Honor. Alice has made arrangements for some young girl from the national school to come in to us for a few hours every day after class to give you a hand.'

'What?' My mother gasped. Have you no servant? No steady servant?'

'We have no need for one,' Vance said. 'Not with only Alice and me. Muggy hardly counts she eats so little and makes so few demands. I assure you Alice is well able to take care of things. Don't look so astonished. Believe me she copes wonderfully well.'

'Copes?' As if it was a word in a foreign language, my mother repeated it uncomprehendingly. '*Copes*?'

'She manages very well. And the man in the yard can do any chores that are too heavy for her. You'll find that you'll be just as good as her.'

'I wonder!' said my mother. 'I'm used to a lot of modern conveniences that I don't expect have found their way here yet. That young one had better be a good strong girl, able and willing too, if this is going to be any kind of vacation for *me*.'

'Calm down, Honor, for heaven's sake,' Vance urged.

Her voice had risen and we were on the outskirts of the town, which seemed to consist entirely of shops, all of which were brightly lighted by large brass lamps hanging on chains from their ceilings. These lamps fully illuminated the interior of the shops but they threw their light no further than the pavement in front of them, and did not reach the middle of the street down which we still continued to parade.

My mother did lower her voice, but now at every shop we passed she wanted to run to the door to say hello and announce she was home again.

'Time enough, time enough, Honor,' Vance counselled. 'Think of Muggy waiting to see you.'

My mother let herself be dragged on, until we came to the Market Square and were about to pass one of the most brightly lit shops of all. 'Are these newcomers to the town?' she asked, as if affronted.

'Not really,' Vance said. 'The Reegans lived outside the town but they came in for a bit of money and bought that place. If you remember it used to be empty, practically falling down. Its windows were boarded up for years.'

'It's not falling down now I see,' my mother said. 'Who is that young man behind the counter?'

'That's Tim. He was at school with me. He's the only son. It's him was responsible for making such a success of the venture.' Vance tried to pull my mother forward by the sleeve. 'There's no need to stare. You'll meet him soon enough.'

My mother let herself be led on a little way but she was looking back over her shoulder. 'Who is the girl outside the counter? The one who is chatting him up? She seems to be making very free with the goods for a customer?'

The girl was very pretty, but my mother was right about

the liberties she was taking. She had just lifted a glass dome from over a round of yellow cheese and pinching off a hunk, she was nibbling it.

'Are they friends? *Special* friends, I mean?' my mother asked.

'Not at all,' Vance said. 'By the way you ought to know *her*, Honor. She's Milly Durkin, a friend of Alice. You must remember her when she was small. She was always in our place. Playing babby house,' he added contemptuously. 'You'll be seeing a lot of her too, I promise you.'

'Oh, is that how the land lies? Is it this Milly who has dimmed the lights of Lisdoonvarna for you?' Before we turned the corner she took another look at Milly.

My heart quickened when we turned into the next street which was long and dark, because it was our street. And when near the end of it high up in the gable-end of a tall house we saw a lighted lamp set in an uncurtained window, I thought my mother was going to faint for joy. 'Oh that light!' she cried. 'In the window of my own little room! I can't believe it's real. I must be dreaming. Pinch me somebody please. To think that tonight I'll be tucked up in my own bed, with my dear old lumpy mattress and my raggedy eiderdown.' She held my hand tighter as if like an electric current, the thrill that went through her might pass into me. Next minute her voice changed. 'There's no light in the shop. Why? Why? Is it shut? What time is it? Was the train late? Oh no, it couldn't have been late because all the rest of the shops are open.' She was becoming increasingly anguished. 'Oh my God,' she said then. 'There's no light in the upstairs drawing-room. There's something wrong.' She swung around to Vance and grabbed his shoulders, shaking him violently. 'Why didn't you tell me? What's the matter? It's Muggy isn't it? She's ill? Bedridden? Oh why wasn't I told? Why didn't you tell me? Tell me *now*.'

Vance shook off her grip on him. 'Muggy is as fit as a fiddle, Honor, but she's not getting younger you must realize, and she keeps to her room most of the time, almost all of the time I should say. We don't use the big drawing-room any more. As for the shop, we close it earlier now. I told you I'd made changes. That's one of them.'

'But why?'

Vance hesitated. 'I was certain Alice had written to you about all this. We've given up the grocery and other unprofitable lines. We've only kept on hardware and we no longer operate that on a retail basis. We go in entirely now for wholesale.'

My mother relaxed somewhat, but she still kept us standing. 'Tell me more about Muggy. Prepare me. I could not bear the shock of seeing a great change in her. Has she aged a lot?' She was almost sobbing. 'I would have thought that the big drawing-room would have been lit up for my homecoming, even if you don't use it as much as formerly.' She stared down the street. The whole house seems dark. Are you sure you're not keeping something back from me?'

'Honor! Will you please give up this inquisition. There is absolutely nothing wrong. I did try to tell you about some of the changes as we were coming through the town but you kept interrupting. When we went into the wholesale trade we naturally needed more storage space and it had to be somewhere dry and safe. You know yourself the condition of the sheds, even in your day they were in bad repair, I should say gone beyond repair. The only available space was the upstairs drawing-room.'

'But Muggy loved the drawing-room. How could you have deprived her of it?'

'Muggy was quite amenable to the change. After all, it

wasn't much use to her when she couldn't go in there to enjoy it. She's more than content with her own room. Wait till you see it. You seem to have forgotten, Muggy's room is at the back and the light doesn't show from the street. I assure you it's lit up like a bazaar. She insisted in bringing in almost every lamp in the place in your honour. And of course as you can imagine, when we were dismantling the drawing-room we brought as many of her treasures into her room as would fit. She's surrounded by things she loves.' Vance had got more confident as he spoke. 'Her bedroom is where she holds court now,' he finished gaily and was preparing to move forward again.

'Well, if she's happy I suppose that's all that matters,' my mother said vaguely. She herself had still made no move to go on. 'What about Alice? Didn't she raise any objections to this – what word did you use – this dismantling of the drawing-room.'

Vance laughed. 'It was mainly her idea. You see you haven't heard half the story yet. We refurbished the small downstairs parlour.'

'*What*,' my mother fairly shouted this time.

'Yes. We had it redecorated and that's where she entertains her friends. We managed to fit in a lot more of the furniture from upstairs, including of course the piano. The rest of the stuff had to go up in one of the lofts. The lofts are dry enough but they would be too inconvenient for the storage of stock.'

'One last question,' my mother said and she put a foot forward as if ready to proceed to the house. 'What about that tribe of – '

'Ah, those spongers. You've seen the last of them. Even before we gave up the grocery I got rid of them. It didn't take me long I can tell you. Their custom was never worth a penny in view of the nuisance they were. To say nothing of what they cost us in hospitality. In the last years of Foggy's life we were the laughing stock of the town. Everyone knew that mob was codding us up to our eyeballs, making use of us without buying much more than a couple of plugs of tobacco or a few bags of boiled sweets, which, needless to say, were entered in the ledger, while they dispensed their real custom elsewhere, paying for those purchases in cash of course.'

'I suppose you were right,' my mother said. 'I can't see how you managed it, though.'

'It was the easiest thing in the world. I simply wrote off their long-term debts, burned the old ledgers and told them to take themselves to blazes and never come back again.'

'Oh was that wise?' The question broke from my mother involuntarily.

'Come on, Honor, and judge for yourself,' Vance said and he drew her towards the house, where we could now see that the hall-door was open letting out a stream of light. The light acted on my mother like a magnet. She darted away from us and like a young girl ran to the door.

'Muggy, Muggy, Muggy. Darling Muggy, I'm home,' we heard her call out as she disappeared into the house. When we ourselves arrived on her heels there was no sign of anyone in the little hallway and only a distant sound of voices somewhere in the upper regions.

A second later those distant voices were drowned out by a ra-ta-tat of footsteps coming down the street, and through the hall door that was still open the girl we had seen in Reegan's shop burst in upon us. Her cheeks were flaming. 'Is it true what I've just heard?' she demanded angrily, addressing herself to Vance.

'How do I know what you heard?' Vance said, but I felt somehow that he did know.

'Oh you make me sick,' said the girl. 'I've just been told that Alice is being packed off to stay with Regina? For how long, I'd like to know?'

'I have no idea,' Vance said, 'but I don't see how it concerns you, Milly.'

'You don't? Oh Vance, you really are a fool. What about our sing-songs down here in the evenings in the little parlour. You surely don't expect me to come down here if Alice is not at home. You know it was on her I was supposed to be calling.'

'And wasn't it?' Vance asked.

'Oh Vance!' The girl was getting more and more exasperated. 'It's a good thing I know you don't mean what you say.'

'What makes you so sure I don't?'

'Because I know you.'

'Or think you do?' My uncle had changed so much I hardly recognized him, he was so severe and forbidding and his voice so cold. 'Who told you anyway?' he asked.

'Tim Reegan. Alice sent him a note earlier this evening and I may as well let you know he wasn't too pleased about it.'

'Rubbish, that pair are like Siamese twins. They are in agreement about everything. I'm sure they discussed it when the suggestion first arose. They are on too good a footing for anyone or anything to create trouble between them.'

'Unlike you and me? Is that what you are really trying to say, Vance?'

'Put it how you like, Milly. All I'm concerned about is that you picked a bad moment for making a scene. Honor has only just arrived. We've just come from the train.'

'I know. I heard your voices when you were coming down the street.' Here Milly vouchsafed me a glance. 'Is this the child?' She didn't smile at me or say anything. Indeed the sight of me gave her a new grievance. 'Even if Alice was not going away, your precious sister Honor might have put an end to our larks anyway, claiming we'd keep the child awake or some such excuse.'

'That's most unfair of you, Milly. And most unlikely. My sister Honor plays the piano better than either you or Alice.'

'Is that so? And what does she play I'd like to know. Mendelssohn's "Spring Song"?'

'What matter if she does? If I understand you right your only objection to the absence of Alice is that without her the proper proprieties would not be preserved. Well, Honor would be a substitute for her.'

Milly reflected on that for a moment. 'That could be true, but I think you are leaving something out of account. Your sister Honor, a matron, might not approve of everything that goes on in your parlour as the evening advances. And what about Tim. He isn't likely to enjoy playing gooseberry for you and me. In spite of what you say about them, I think Alice is taking a big risk going off like this just when everyone is beginning to talk about wedding bells ringing out for her and Tim any day now.'

'Oh give over your hypocrisy, Milly Durkin. It's not for Alice's sake that you don't like to see her go.'

Milly tossed her head. 'If so there's no harm in that. We're all entitled to look out for ourselves in this life and I'm going to miss the good times we've been having down here.' She moved closer to him and she gave him a smile that I thought was very sweet. 'Won't you?' She asked almost in a whisper. 'How long is she going to be gone anyway?' She asked more crisply when Vance remained silent.

'I don't know and I don't care,' Vance said.

Milly moved back a bit from him. 'Whose idea was it in the first place? I bet it was your old mother, trying to interfere once more, as she was well known to do in the case of all your other sisters, only this time it would be positively criminal to get between Alice and the best catch in the county.' Suddenly a new idea had struck her. 'I forgot that she's no fool. I suppose she realizes, like you said yourself, that no one could come between those two, so perhaps it's you and me she wants to keep apart. After all if Alice got married there'd be only you left, and if you – '

If my uncle Vance was cold before this, he was now icy cold.

'Milly Durkin, do you seriously think that poor old Muggy is the only obstacle to your catching me in your little butterfly net? You flatter yourself if that's what you think.'

As if he'd struck her Milly put her hands up to her face. 'Oh Vance, Vance!' she moaned. 'What a thing to say! What a cruel, cruel thing to say. And to think how I loved you all my life, or thought I did, and believed you loved me, and that it would be only a matter of time till you realized it and that – '

I couldn't hear the rest of the sentence because she had taken her hands from her face, which was wet with tears and she ran out blindly into the dark street.

Vance opened the parlour door and went in closing the door after him. He did not give me as much as a look.

The conversation I heard that first night in Ireland was the first of its kind I had ever heard, where the thoughts and feelings of the speakers were buried far below their words, like plants with sparse, innocuous leaves that have roots in the ground are deadly poison. I stood in the narrow hallway not knowing what to do when someone came tripping lightly down the stairs. 'So *this* is where you are,' said my aunt Alice. 'I thought you were with your mother up in Muggy's room. I only came down because I thought I heard Vance and Milly quarrelling.'

'They were,' I said.

'Oh dear. They'll never get sense, that pair. In front of you too. And on your first night here. Shame on them.' She glanced at the closed door of the parlour. 'Where are they?'

'Milly went home. *He's* in there,' I said pointing at the parlour. 'I think he forgot about me.'

'A good job I found you!' Alice said. 'If your uncle forgot you, it's my belief your mother has forgotten that you were ever born!' But I knew she was joking. She went on joking. 'Your mother is closeted up in Muggy's room and they are talking to beat the band, both together at the same time. To hear them you'd think there would be no tomorrow, that Doomsday was at hand. But I bet you're longing to put your head on the pillow.' She paused as if to ponder something. 'I wonder if I ought to bring you up to let your grandmother see you, or wait until morning when your mother has you all spruced up. Tomorrow I think,' she said decisively and picking me up she cuddled me close and went to carry me to bed when something scraped my cheek, I drew back with a start, and then I saw that what I had always thought were the sculptured wings of her hair were the loops of a bow, her famous taffeta bow. Her hair itself was fine and soft and it lay as tight to her head as sewing silk to its spool. It, too, was in a grown-up bun only hers was no bigger than a button. Everything about her was neat and simple and sweet and I felt like crying at the thought of her going away next day.

'Why are you going?' I asked sadly.

'I'll tell you when you're in bed. I'll sit on the foot of the bed and we'll have a little chat because I'll probably be gone when you wake. Regina lives very far away and it takes a whole day to get there.'

'I know,' I said, but we had reached the first landing and I struggled out of her arms to let her see that I knew my way. 'My mother showed me the light in our window,' I said, but Alice caught me and held me back.

'Oh dear!' she said. 'I suppose I should have put Honor in her own room. It never occurred to me. It can't matter much though when she's only going to be here so short a time.' She opened a door on the landing where we stood. 'This is the room I got ready for you,' she said, 'It's much bigger than your mother's old room. I only moved up there when Muggy got incapacitated, in case she might need me during the night.'

It was a lovely room. I surveyed it from the big bed on to which she dumped me down. There was a fire blazing up the chimney and my mother's carnations were already in a vase, although they were so clearly on their last legs.

'Oh I wish you weren't going away,' I said again.

'I'll be back in a few days. I wouldn't be going at all only Muggy felt that it would be nice for Regina to have a little help just now. You know she's – ' I nodded. 'And, as for me, it's a perfect opportunity to get a change of air while your mother is here to take care of Muggy. I've scarcely been out of the house since first Regina and then Lally took the law into their own hands and skedaddled.' She laughed and I laughed too. Quite suddenly Alice asked, 'What were Vance and Milly quarrelling about?'

'About you,' I said, 'Milly told – '

'Oh, don't tell me. I know she's mad at me for going.'

'She said Tim – '

'Oh I'm sure she tried to use Tim to further her own plans. Milly is my friend but she can be very disloyal at times.'

'She's in love with my uncle Vance, isn't she?' I asked.

'Ssh, ssh,' Alice said, but gently, and she laid a finger across my lips. 'I don't know what is the custom in America, but in Ireland we don't make free with the word love. We'd put it another way. We'd say Milly *likes* Vance. That's how we'd put it.'

Taking care to use her own words and place the emphasis on the right word, I dared another question.

'You *like* Tim Reegan too, don't you,' I said, 'and he *likes* you.' When Alice blushed I got bolder. 'That's why he's cross because you're going away.'

'Cross with me? Tim.' Alice looked slightly surprised, then she laughed again. 'I suppose that was more of Milly's nonsense. Tim is *glad* I'm going, glad I'm getting a little holiday. We talked about it long ago, the first day we got your mother's letter announcing her arrival. He's perfectly happy about it.' Seeing that I was not convinced she bent and whispered in my ear, 'Tim and I have an understanding if you know what that means.'

'You're engaged?' I sat up all excited, 'Can I be your bridesmaid?'

'Ssh,' she said again, but I knew she hadn't really minded my saying it at all. 'We're not exactly engaged, but it's almost the same thing. He gave me a lovely old ring that belonged to his mother, but I don't wear it on my finger because there are a lot of practicalities to be disposed of before we make our intentions public.'

'Muggy?' I suggested.

'Only partly. Poor Muggy! It would be very hard for me to leave her in the hands of a stranger, especially since she can't have much longer to enjoy life. Tim is in full agreement with me that we must show concern for her. No dear, Muggy is not the real problem. It's Vance. Tim is his best friend and he worries about him as much as I do. We'd both like to see him settled before we get married ourselves, of course, if Muggy were to be suddenly called to her reward, he could always come and live with us. It wouldn't be an ideal situation though. He wouldn't like it either. Such arrangements are rarely satisfactory.'

'Why don't you try to get him to marry Milly when she likes him so much. And I think he *likes* her too, no matter how nasty he was to her tonight.'

'My goodness, you are a little fox. That's exactly what Tim and I would like to see happen. In fact we are confident he'll marry her in the end. If only she'd stop chasing him, she'd have him eating out of her hand. Instead she's been running after him like a little dog ever since we were small, although she used to pretend, even then, that it was to play with me she was coming down here all the time.'

'Babby house?'

'Oh you are a real little Big Ears, aren't you? Vance said that I'm sure. Poor Milly. Not that I see any harm in her wanting a home and children. It's a natural longing for any girl – any woman I mean. Milly's mistake is in pushing too hard for what she wants, and in the wrong way. It's the man who must make the pace, or at least think it's him that's making it, although there are subtle ways in which a woman can get her way – sometimes. I often wonder if Milly isn't too overpowering for Vance. She makes no allowance for his health and he's not very strong as I suppose you know. He could have reservations about taking on the responsibilities of a wife and family.'

I thought about that, but I didn't think it a big factor in

the situation. 'Maybe Milly wouldn't mind him dying as long as she had him for a while,' I said.

'Oh hush, hush, child,' Alice said, more harshly than the other times. 'Don't say things like that! Who spoke of anyone dying? What an idea! It's just that Vance's store of strength is slender and he has to be careful not to overdo things. And now you must go to sleep. I'm going to say goodnight to you and quench the lamp.'

I was asleep before she was out of the room. Late in the night I thought I heard herself and my mother talking in our room. I thought they were arguing about a bed or an eiderdown but I was too drowsy to hear properly and I went back to sleep.

When I woke next morning, my mother's side of the bed was empty, and even through the wads and wads of old faded wallpaper, I could hear her voice up in my grandmother's room. She was still catching up on all that had happened at home during her exile. I dressed myself and went downstairs where I found a plate of bread and butter and a glass of milk that must have been meant for me. When I'd eaten I made my way out to the shop, only it wasn't like a shop at all. It was like a warehouse and my uncle Vance was kneeling in the middle of the floor unpacking large crates of cups and saucers and statues and mousetraps and a whole lot of other things, to repack them in small parcels and put labels on them. He was covered with sawdust and his clothes were stuck all over with wood shavings but he looked very happy. He invited me to help but I was afraid I'd break something so after a while I wandered out into the yard.

The yard was exactly like I expected. So was the garden although I couldn't get into it because the gate was too heavy for me to push open. Standing on tippy toes I saw that the houses and shops to either side of ours had the same ramifications of sheds in their yards, although ours were a bit more broken down and had rusty corrugated roofs instead of slates. I thought to myself that it would be as easy to walk around the town on the top of those roofs as it was for my mother and the aunts to walk around the rampart wall.

I was going back into the house when I noticed that the door of a loft over one of the sheds hung half open because a hinge was missing, and up in the loft I caught a glimpse of all sorts of furniture, up-ended tables and chairs and pictures and mirrors. I saw one mirror that had brass candelabras on each side of it. The cast-offs from the old drawing-room! I nearly died with excitement. If I could get up there and turn things right side up and rearrange them I might make a drawing-room in that loft. What a surprise my mother would get when I'd take her up and show her. There would be no piano but I didn't think that a great loss. My drawing-room would be an upstairs one too, I thought with increasing excitement until I noticed that the treads of the wooden ladder leading up there were worn and greenmouldy, and when I went to go up, they creaked terribly and I saw that the handrail only went up a bit of the way. Then I saw that at the top, where they counted most, the last three steps were gone. That would be a serious obstacle. I was wondering how I could mend them when I heard my mother's voice below me.

'What on earth are you doing? That ladder is rotten. You could be killed. Come down at once. I saw you eat the bread and butter I left for you, but when that girl arrives after school, she'll give us all a hot meal – I hope.'

I don't remember my first meeting with my grand-mother very clearly. I was never going to see much of her.

My mother monopolized most of her company. When I was brought for a visit to her room, my mother kept urging her not to let me tire her, not to tax her energies.

My first meeting with Annie, the girl got in to help in the hours after school, was very nice but she had to work very hard and she said she hadn't time for talking. When I offered to help her she said it wouldn't be proper.

'Why don't they send you to school?' she asked.

'I suppose it's not worthwhile. We're only here on a visit.'

Overhead just then there were sounds of cases being dragged along the floor as my mother was moving us into her old room.

'It sounds like a long visit,' Annie said.

The day dragged to an end and I was more lonely than I'd ever been in America. I fully expected the next day to be the same, and the next and the next but in the morning when I was standing at the hall-door looking aimlessly into the street, a small round knob of a head popped out the door of a shop across the street, and then another identical to it, and I saw two little ladies dressed from head to foot in black, beckoning me. Politeness would appear to demand that I go over to them. They were very nice and they put me sitting up on the counter and brought out a plate of biscuits and showed me their cat, and I told them all about our house in America. But when I went home my mother was furious and Vance wasn't pleased either.

'I forgot to warn you,' my mother said, 'In Ireland people are only nice to children in order to inveigle information out of them.'

'They said they were our cousins,' I protested.

'All the more reason to keep away from them,' Vance said. 'If those two gossips try to coax you over there again tell them you have to go up the town on a message.'

I'd never been told to tell a lie before and in our town in America I wasn't allowed to go up or down the street, even to school without a big girl with me. Vance didn't know it but he had all unknowingly given me a passport to visit the whole town. In every street people rushed out to say they knew who I was, and kiss me and be nice to me! In no time at all I was going more familiarly from house to house in that town than from room to room in my grandmother's.

My mother and Vance were wrong about people wanting to get information. They were really, truly, interested in our family and they listened avidly to everything I told them. They said I was a scream and that I ought to be on the stage the way I was such a good mimic. The questions they asked were all the same, all only polite enquiries. When was my father coming home? Was my mother really going to buy a house in Dublin? How was Regina? And how long was Alice going to have to stay away? It was Alice they asked about mostly. They said such nice things about her, that she was so gentle, so unselfish and that she deserved the best.

So, after all, the days and weeks passed quickly. I didn't get to know other children because they were at school all day and at night they had to do their homework, but I was shy with children of my own age. I was quite happy with the grown-ups. Or at least I was happy until the days began to get long and the bright evenings came. Then suddenly the town that had seemed like one big house and the people one big warm-hearted family began to seem confined and stuffy, and I began to get lonely for the walks on which my father used to take me in the woods behind us back home.

I confessed this to Annie one day as she was black-leading the grate in the parlour. She took time to sit back on her hunkers for a minute.

'You used to pick *violets*?' she asked. 'Violets don't grow wild. Are you sure they weren't primroses? There are millions of primroses in the ramparts.'

'How do you know?' I was awe-stricken. 'Nobody ever goes in there. Isn't it a bad place?' Annie looked contemptuously at me.

'Are you mad?' She asked. 'Where do you think me and my friends would play in summer if it wasn't in there?' She glanced at the window where the spring sunlight twinkled on the glass panes. 'I'd be there now if I didn't have to work here. And it isn't only children that go in there. Lots of people go. People from Dublin are always coming down there – even in winter – with notebooks to take down things about the old ruins. And when the fishing season starts fellows from Galway are always in there fishing in the stream.' I was dumb with amazement which Annie took for disbelief because she knit her brows trying to think of more convincing arguments for the popularity of the place that was clearly her favourite haunt. 'And lovers. I forgot to mention them. It's a great place for lovers.'

'Annie. Could I go in there?' I asked almost in a whisper.

'Who's to stop you?'

'Without being seen I mean?'

'Nobody seems to ask where you are when you're out, do they?'

Within an hour I had found a gap in the old wall in a back lane where there were only very poor people living and where most of the cottages were tumbled down. I climbed up easily and dropped down into the forbidden domain. It was true there were a lot of nettles and thistles and I could see rubbish had been thrown across the wall here and there but the nettles grew through it and over it and concealed a lot. The main thing was that the nettles were only just alongside the wall and everywhere else they had been trampled down by people's feet. The places was as criss-crossed with paths as the public gardens in Boston.

As I went deeper in there were groves of trees with stretches of the tall, thin, brilliantly green grass that only grows in woodland places. And then I saw my first primrose. I wouldn't dream of picking it, it was so beautiful, until I looked around and saw that Annie was right, on all sides there were millions and millions of them and I began to pick a bunch, a big, big bunch, until I was almost scared to death by a voice right behind me.

'Pretty aren't they?' Said an old woman I had not seen approaching. She was very old and she was carrying a bundle of twigs tied with twisted grass across her back. To rest herself she left down the twigs. 'I know you,' she said, 'You're the little girl from America that's living here now.'

I sprang up. 'Oh please, please don't tell anyone you saw me. My mother and my uncle told me never to come in here.'

The old woman gave a funny laugh like the cackle of a hen. 'God give them sense,' she said. 'They might as well try to stop the birds from flying in here than try to keep out a normal child. And some that are not children too,' she said and she winked. 'But it's nice to see a little girl picking primroses. I used to love to pick big bunches long ago before I got old and stiff.' She looked at my bunch. 'Pick some leaves too and put a collarette around them and you'll have a lovely posy. But excuse me for asking – what are you going to do with them if you say you're not supposed to be in here? If you take them home they'll ask at once where you got them.'

I hadn't thought of that.

'You could say you got them under the hedges on a road outside the town but that would be a lie. And you were probably told not to go out in the country either.'

'That's right. In case I'd be chased by a bull or a ram.'

The old woman laughed at that, but she didn't say why. She returned to my problem. 'Of course you could give them to the nun in charge of putting flowers on the altar in the chapel, only she might tell your people. Nuns are terrible for meddling in other people's business on account of having nothing to do themselves. I'm afraid, child, you'll just have to find a nice mossy place and lay them down to wither back into the earth like we all have to do some day. They'd have to wither anyway whether they were picked or not.'

'As well as that I don't know the nuns,' I said. 'I don't go to school.'

'God bless my soul! I thought that nowadays there were inspectors going around forcing poor parents to send children to school whether it suited them to do so or not. In my day parents were let keep their children at home if they were more needed there to mind younger children or an old person, or a sick relative.' She shook her head. 'Come on I'll help you find a nice place for your posy.'

I hated to leave them behind but held them up to my nose to smell their perfume before I parted with them.

'Primroses have no scent at all. Did you not know that?' the old woman said taking them from me and laying them down for me in spite of her stiff back. 'Primroses only smell of the earth, but that's a smell we may as well get used to sooner or later.'

'You know an awful lot of things,' I couldn't help remarking.

She gave her funny little cackle again.

'All I ever learned, I learned in here,' she said. 'I learned from the birds and the flowers and the bees and the rabbits and even from the little fishes in the stream forever darting about attending to their own affairs, never idle for a moment.' We made our way back to pick up her twigs and after she hoisted them on her back she glanced around her. Her face was so old I couldn't tell whether she was happy or sad. 'It was in here, in this place, I met my young husband that's dead this thirty years,' she said. Unmistakably I saw then she was happy by the way her face lit up. 'That's one reason I like wandering around here specially on spring evenings like this because when I see some handsome young fellow with a fishing rod maybe, or with his sweetheart, it makes me think of my own man. My eyes are not as good as they used to be and some people might not see any blessing in that, but often when I see young lovers running into each other's arms I can pretend that it's us two, my man and me, and that we are young again and full of strength and happiness.' She looked around again and so did I. 'We're not likely to see any lovers here at this hour,' she said. 'Times have changed and now most of them wait till it's dusk,' she said in a mildly reproving way. 'They steal in singly from different directions, and search around for secret corners where they'll be out of sight. Either that or else nestle down in a place where the grass is so high you'd be in danger of stumbling over them, if it wasn't for hearing them whispering and giggling. Me and my man never sat down in here for fear of the damp. Where there are trees the damp sleeps in the ground, even on hot summer days. Not but today is a nice, fine, dry day. You could chance washing blankets today,' she said, thoughtfully. 'But even on a day like this, my man and me would be content to walk around, keeping to the path, linked arm in arm, proud both of us to be seen together. We never talked much either, but there's no such thing as silence between lovers. Every sound, every stir, the fall of a leaf, the chirp of a bird, the brush of its wings against a little branch, the hum of the bees, the dip of a reed into the stream, when a mayfly lights on top of the water, all, all those sounds are voices speaking for lovers. And for children. Don't feel bad about the primroses.' She shifted her bundle to balance its weight. 'Goodbye, dear child,' she said as she shuffled away.

I didn't stay long after her. I saw lots of people, young boys fishing in the stream, people gathering faggots, and a tight knot of city people with cameras taking pictures of the ruins. And, as the old woman said, I would have tripped over a couple lying in the grass only I smelled the smoke of their cigarettes and avoided them. I saw lots and lots of people, and since some of them were people I knew, who might know me, I evaded them. I wished I didn't have to do that, but I was afraid they might tell on me and I might never again set foot in my new-found paradise.

It was to safeguard my paradise I decided to go home earlier than usual just in case I might be missed. The trouble was I couldn't be sure of the path by which I had entered. Taking a chance, I climbed up on a heap of fallen stones inside a nice easy gap, and I had just thrown my leg over the top, when I saw the gap did not lead into the lane but into one of the main streets, and strolling leisurely down the street was my uncle Vance into whose astonished eyes I was forced to stare.

'What the hell are you doing up there?' he yelled, 'You know that's no fit place for you or any proper person. Come down at once.' Disregarding the height from which I'd have to drop, he offered me no assistance. 'Wait till your mother hears about this escapade,' he said. 'Maybe she'll believe what's being said, that you're being let run wild all over the town.'

'Do you have to tell her, Uncle Vance?' I whispered.

'Most certainly,' he said. 'Maybe it will bring her to her senses.'

My shame gave way to a brash hope. 'Will you make her send me to school?

He gave a queer laugh. 'Is it to provide her with further grounds for prolonging her so-called visit? Is that what you mean?'

Then, prodding me in the back with a malacca cane he'd recently begun to carry, he drove me before him through the streets.

My mother when she was told was more incredulous than angry.

'Don't you believe me?' Vance yelled at her.

'Of course I believe you, Vance. There's no need to raise your voice. It's just hard to accept that a daughter of mine would put her foot in that unhealthy, that unsavoury place.' Then she gave her attention to me. 'How did you get in there? How long were you inside? What were you doing? You must be stung all over by nettles. Show me your legs. Let me tell you, Miss, if you've got nettle rash you'll learn a lesson you won't forget in a hurry. Wait until you're in bed tonight, between the warm blankets, that's when nettle rash really flares up. You'll richly deserve it. What about me though? If anything happened to you, anything dreadful I mean, how could I face your father? Don't you realize, didn't we tell you, only bad people go in there, people who don't want anyone to know what they're up to, people who don't want their doings brought out in the open.'

'That's not true,' I cried. 'I saw lots of ordinary people in there, *nice* prople, people you *know*.' I paused. 'Friends of yours.'

My mother and Vance looked at each other for guidance. 'Friends of ours? Name them,' my mother demanded.

'Well, for one, there was Tim Reegan. I saw him.'

'Nonsense,' Vance said. 'What would Tim be doing in there?'

'Oh don't mind the child,' my mother said. 'She probably mistook someone else for him. Or he might have had some necessity for going in there, such as to take stock of its disgusting condition to organize a campaign for cleaning it up, putting it to proper use like we spoke about. You said he was a progressive young man. One way or another the presence in it of a single, isolated person of respectability doesn't make the place respectable.' She swung around to face me. 'Who else did you see? You said you saw lots of people. Name them then!'

I must, I think, at this point, have had a qualm, a terrible intimation that I was disloyal, because I would certainly have considered it disloyal if anyone had told them they'd seen *me* in there, but Vance had begun to shake me by the shoulders so hard he shook another name out of me.

'Milly Durkin,' I said. I was instantly aware I had created havoc.

Vance went white as chalk. 'Not with Tim? Not together?'

My mother put one hand across my mouth and with the other she caught Vance by the arm. 'Oh Vance. Try not to read too much into this, Vance, for God's sake. They were probably talking about Alice.'

'Like hell they were!' Vance said.

'Oh Vance,' my mother let go of me and tried to put her

arms around my uncle. 'Don't hide your feelings if you are upset. Not from me! It will only make the hurt worse.'

'Oh shut up, you,' Vance said, 'I told you before, Honor, you can't put back the clock.'

To me he was extraordinarily kind. 'This has nothing to do with you, child,' he said. 'In a way we are in your debt.' Then he sort of hummed a few words I didn't understand. I think that he did't really know he was saying them out loud. 'So the honey bees have swarmed elsewhere,' he said. Then he raised his voice. 'Alice must be told,' he said. 'She must be given a chance to come back.'

'But will she? Has it not occurred to you that Alice may have too much pride to come running back because of what, after all, may be only surmise. Personally, I'd like to think she'd have more dignity.'

'Is that so? I suppose it all depends on how deeply she loves him – and on her stamina. She'll have to come home eventually, and if the worst comes to the worst, she may as well face the music now as later. I can't help feeling that the sight of her might bring Reegan back to his senses.'

My mother's face had changed. 'That would suit you nicely too,' she snapped at him. 'Alice would be fighting your battles for you as well as her own. You know all this is your own fault. You've played fast and loose with Milly Durkin as long as it suited you.'

Unexpectedly, Vance sank on to a chair. He sort of caved in. I thought he was going to cry. 'You know, or you ought to know, Honor, that I have enough battles to fight without bringing any more on myself. And you know who is the real one at fault in this miserable situation.'

'If you mean Muggy – ?' My mother was up in arms at once but she wasn't let continue.

'I don't mean Muggy. Muggy may have decided your

destiny, and by all accounts her choice wasn't a bad one as far as we could judge at the time. But she undid Magdalene's happiness, and if they hadn't stood up to her she'd have interfered in the lives of Regina and Lally. But she's too old now to rule the roost. No, it's you, Honor, it's you who is responsible for the fate of Alice, whatever that fate is to be. If you hadn't hung on here she'd have had to come back after the short rest she originally planned.'

'But Regina loved having her and – '

'Regina did not know all the circumstances. She didn't know that you'd make no attempt to find a house except for a few half-hearted day trips to Dublin when you spent all the time with Lally. Might I be permitted to ask, even at this late hour, have you any real intention of buying a house. Did your husband really put the money for it in the bank?'

'How dare you insinuate otherwise?'

'Alright, keep your hair on. Tell me one thing only. How does your husband take your dilly-dallying?'

'He is in no hurry, he is not pressing me, if that's what you want to know. He told me on the wharf at Boston when we were leaving that I was to take my time and make sure I got a suitable house. His very words were that it would be better to be sure than sorry. He's suffering no inconvenience I can assure you. He has arranged to take his meals in the lodging house where he lived as a bachelor for thirty years. He hasn't sold our house yet either, or the furniture.' Then she gave her gay little laugh that never fully revealed whether or not she was joking. 'Maybe he's hoping we'll change our minds and go back.'

Vance looked oddly at her.

'Maybe it's the other way round. Maybe your husband is glad to be rid of you and you've come back here to be a cuckoo in the nest.'

I had only barely understood the first part of what he said, and nothing at all of the last but I knew something was wrong and that it concerned me as much as any of them. I burst out crying.

My mother dropped all argument and tried to stop me. 'If Muggy hears this it will worry her to death,' she said, speaking not to me but to Vance.

It was then Vance said something I never thought to hear.

'To hell with Muggy too,' he said. 'It's Alice we've got to think about now. She must be got back at once. Tim Reegan may be weak but he's hardly fool enough to fall for Milly Durkin's coxy-orum, if he is brought face to face with Alice he might come to his senses. There's only one thing puzzles me. Why does Alice not see that if you're home for good then there would no longer be any obstacle in the way of her marrying Tim. Unless – ' Suddenly he grabbed me and began to shake me again. 'Was this your first escapade, or were you inside the ramparts before today?' When I shook my head he let me go. 'I thought perhaps they'd been seen in there on other occasions.'

I knew what he was getting at then. 'Maybe someone else saw them and wrote to Alice?'

'The child could be right,' my mother said crisply.

Vance gave her an ugly look. 'Not you by any chance?' he said but now my mother began to cry. 'I'm sorry. I didn't mean it, Honor. How could I say such a hateful thing to you above all.'

My mother stopped crying. 'You've had good practice being hateful to Milly, or so I've been told,' she said.

Vance closed his eyes to hide the pain in them. 'Well,' he said then in a strange voice, 'this conversation is getting us nowhere. It alters nothing. You are the only one who has the remedy in your hands – if there is ever a remedy for a lost cause. You've got to stop hanging on here upside down like a bat in a barn. If you value your immortal soul you'll take your child and get out of here this very night. You can stay with Lally for the present. If you need money I'll give it to you.'

My mother made no attempt at defence beyond a weak enquiry about who would look after Muggy.

'I'll take care of that. That young one, Annie, can miss school for a few nights and sleep in the house. Go on now, Honor, start packing. He gave her a push towards the stairs. He didn't have to push me. I had clung to my mother's skirt and I was brought along with my feet barely touching the ground.

We did not leave that night but left first thing next day. We didn't go to Lally, we stopped in a small hotel and within a week my mother had found a house and bought it with the money that really was lodged in her name in the bank. I think she bought the first house she saw and I didn't like it one bit. When my father arrived at the end of the month, I saw he, too, was disappointed when his cab drew up outside our door and he took stock of it from the window before he stepped out and picked me up to throw me up in the air like a ball, the way he used to do at home. I'd got a bit too big for that.

'I've missed so much of you, but we'll make up for it,' he said. To my mother he was like he always was, polite. 'Was this the best you could do with the money?' he asked.

It's near my school,' I intervened and I started to tell him about the convent to which I'd been sent as a day pupil and where I was instantly happy and indeed lastingly so.

When we got inside I was in full spate. My mother, however, drew him aside before he even had a chance to see the house. Something had happened of which I had not been informed. My father was staggered by her news. 'I must say I didn't expect to come home to this. Are you sure? Poor Vance. We'll have to go down there at once. I'll be buying a car anyway so I'll get one today and we'll go first thing in the morning. He'll probably have to be sent to a sanatorium, only for a while I hope, but he might be recommended to go to Switzerland if the money for that can be found. And it can. Your young sister Alice certainly cannot take care of him at home, apart from the danger of contagion.'

'Alice is behaving magnificently,' my mother said.

So she had come back. Nobody told me. Did she make up with Tim I wondered, but when I asked my mother she said sourly that Tim had married Milly two days after I had seen them in the ramparts. When Alice had heard this she vowed she would never come back again but that night Vance had a haemorrhage. Alice came back at once.

It didn't take my father long to buy a car. You might say he took one off the rack, and the morning after his arrival we drove to the west of Ireland.

My mother spoke very little on the journey except for exclamations such as that it would kill Muggy if Vance had to be sent to a sanatorium. She adhered to the suggestion of the local doctor who had proposed a chalet be built in the garden with one side open to the sun by day and to the air at all times. Air, rest and lots of milk was all that was considered necessary.

My father said nothing beyond insisting we wait until we had assessed the situation for ourselves.

The door, when we arrived, was opened by Annie. The chalet, she told us, had already been erected and Vance installed in it, so we went straight out to the garden. The garden looked strange with the scrub and weed mowed down, but Vance looked, to me at least, the same as ever. He was in very good humour. He greeted my mother more effusively than he had greeted her at the station but his words were somewhat cryptic.

'So, Honor, I am playing babby house after all,' he said before giving me his full attention, proffering me all kinds of goodies. 'A piece of cake? An orange? Some chocolates? Take anything you please.' He handed me a biscuit as a starter.

'She's not allowed to eat between meals,' my mother murmured, taking the biscuit out of my hand and putting it back on the plate.

'Since when?' my uncle asked in an odd sort of voice. My mother flushed. 'Can I have it?' I asked putting out my hand. 'No,' Vance said very sharply but the sharpness was not directed at me.

Then Alice appeared. She had a tray of food for Vance and told us there was something prepared for us in the house. I didn't like to stare too hard at her but to me she too was as unchanged as Vance. If anything, she was more animated, and when we went inside, the whole house had a livelier air to it. I think there were visitors upstairs with my grandmother, and I heard a lot of voices in the kitchen. Back in the house my mother began to cry.

'They acted for the best, Honor,' my father said. 'The local doctor knew what he was prescribing. It would have been a needless penance on all concerned to send your brother away. He's too far gone for a sanatorium. And I think he knows it, has in fact known it for a long time. He'll be happy here for what time is left to him. And your poor old mother will have the consolation of seeing that his least desires are granted.' He took my mother in his arms, something I'd never seen him do before. 'The old woman can't have long to go either. It might be a blessing if she went before him.'

My mother pulled away from him. 'Oh, no, no, no,' she sobbed.

'He need not be told about her death, but his could not easily be kept from her.'

Alice at that moment returned. To our astonishment an altercation broke out at once between her and my mother.

'Are you insinuating that we stay in a hotel?' my mother asked. 'Can't we make up our beds if necessary?'

Apparently there were no beds, or more precisely no mattresses.

'The doctor advised burning all bedding,' Alice said.

My father had to come between them. 'Honor,' he reasoned, 'Alice may have some justification for her action. If she hadn't dismantled the rooms, she might have been expected to provide accommodation for all your sisters and their husbands and children whenever they came here. She could have ended up running a hotel as well as a hospital. Don't look so stricken. We have a car. We can easily be back in Dublin before night and we can come and go as often as needed, or as often as you wish.'

That summer my parents went to see Vance every other week. As time advanced I seldom went. I had made friends in school with whom I could stay and it was thought best that I do so.

One day, however, when my father was going to the Galway races, he took me with him and dropped me off to spend the day with Alice.

I was amazed at how the tempo of life had changed in the house. Approaching death had brought back the activity of my mother's youth. Vance's chalet in the garden had become the centre of the town and from that garden, almost all day long laughter spouted upwards and sprayed the air like water from a fountain. Vance had always revelled in company and intended to do so to the last. The hall-door was never shut so visitors for Vance could come and go at their or his own sweet will, except at meal times. Alice had issued an ordnance that the invalid must be left alone at meal times in the hope that he'd do more than pick at the delicacies prepared for him. Nobody disobeyed this wise decree.

My father was the only one to voice an awkward question. 'Has his friend Reegan ever come to see him?'

'Certainly not,' my mother replied.

'Or Milly?' my father asked.

'Don't mention her name. Do you think Alice would tolerate that? It was Milly she blamed in the first place and quite rightly, but she's got over all that.'

Whatever about Milly, deep down we all felt Vance must be hurt that Tim never came to see him although he never mentioned his name. And then on that day my father dropped me off there, I was witness to a strange thing. Alice had brought out my poor uncle's midday meal but she had forgotten to retrieve the tray. We were sitting laughing about unimportant things in the past when she remembered and sprang up but in order to continue our conversation I went with her.

Halfway across the yard, although I was behind her I thought I heard voices in the garden. Alice certainly did. She stopped abruptly and motioned me to do likewise. Putting her finger to her lips for silence she stood deadly still and I was amazed at how she was transformed by what she heard. The next thing we both heard was the sound of someone scrambling up on the top of our garden wall and from that on to the roof of our shed, running from there

like my childhood fantasy along the roofs of the neighbouring sheds.

'Do you know who that was?' Alice asked of me in a
voice I now know to have been tremulous. 'It was Tim.
And I could tell by the way he and Vance were talking that
it wasn't his first visit. He must have been coming to see
him across the roof like that ever since we built the chalet.
Oh I knew he could not have been heartless enough to stay
away. It was just that he didn't want anyone to know.
Above all Milly! Do you realize what this means?' she said,
and then her face lit up with so strange a light of happiness I
was frightened by it. 'You don't realize but I heard what
they were saying, their last few words, and I know now
what I always guessed that she stole him from me. He and
Vance must have been talking about when they were
young, when we were all young, and he was doing his best
to cheer Vance up with hopes he must have known were
empty and vain. "You'll see Vance," he said, "Those good
times will come back. Before the summer is gone, you'll be
up and about again." But Vance knew better.' Tears
gushed into Alice's eyes. 'Poor Vance! He chastised Tim,
gently, gently but firmly. "You can't delude me, Tim, I'll
be gone long before the summer is gone, I'll be gone."' In
the grip of a strange excitement my aunt caught hold of me,
'And do you know what Tim said – his last words before he
went back over the sheds? "It's well for you, Vance," he
said. Those were his very words. "It's well for you. I'd
gladly change places with you."' As she spoke it was as if a
fever was mounting in her, and consuming her in its fires,
fires that like a martyr she fed with a fuel within her. She
closed her eyes for a moment. Then she opened them to see
that I understood the full story. 'Do you realize what that
means? It means I was right. Tim is unhappy. He has been

unhappy from the start. Terribly, terribly, terribly unhappy.' Her elation made her tremble and in the blindness
that accompanied it I was able to run out of the house to
where my father was waiting for me, impatient to be on the
road to Dublin before dark.

Three days later a telegram arrived for us.

My mother received it but couldn't open it. She handed
it to my father. 'It's Vance! He's gone,' she said.

'It's not Vance,' my father said slowly in utter disbelief.
'It's Tim Reegan. Blood poisoning. How could he have got
that? And how could it have been neglected?'

*   *   *

The dead bell was tolling as we drove into the town. There
was a conflict between my parents as to whether we should
go to Reegan's house or straight to the chapel. 'To neither,'
my father said, 'we'll go to the old home. Alice may need
support.'

Alice was in no need of support. All the aunts had
assembled accompanied by their husbands and children.
They were evidently expecting us, awaiting our arrival.
Calling Alice, who was upstairs, they made our arrival the
signal for a massed departure.

When Alice had come down the stairs I had noticed
nothing unusual, nor in the bustle to leave did the others,
until my mother drew a sharp breath and accosted her.

'What is the meaning of this?' she asked, staring at her
sister's hair. For instead of the brown taffeta bow to which
we were all accustomed, Alice wore a bow of deep black
crêpe. My mother was almost hysterical. 'What are you
attempting to do? Make a show of yourself? Make a show
of all of us? A public display? Go upstairs at once and

change that bow. You may have reason to mourn him, but you have no rights to do so.'

'I have the right,' Alice said, and she fastened her eyes on me. 'Tell them what you heard him say,' she ordered me.

My mother appealed to my father. 'Do something!' she said.

My father quietly stepped over to Alice and unpinned the black bow.

I put my hands over my eyes. There was something shocking in the way she was transformed. She was denuded, that was the only word for how she appeared to me. Dazed we stared at her as she stood for a moment looking at us and then ran up the street to the chapel. We began to follow her, slowly as if we were following the hearse, except my father.

'Let the child stay back,' he said. 'She can sit with Vance. Does he know about Tim?'

'He must have heard the dead bell,' Regina said, 'but he's too low to know for whom it tolls. People thought the two coffins would be before the altar together, side by side. They were thinking the two sides of the nave doors would have to be opened.'

Yet Vance did not die that night. He lived for another week. My grandmother lived long enough to spare him her death but suffer his. The brothers-in-law took control of the practical matters. The business was let to a small merchant who allowed Alice to live on in the dwelling quarters overhead.

I was not brought to Vance's funeral. Alice made some kind of scene at the Reegan funeral and anyway I was engrossed in the activities of my new school, the studies and games and friendship of other children, things I had never enjoyed before. I did not often see my Aunt Alice after that but whenever I did the lack of a bow on her hair filled me with an odd mixture of pity and revulsion. And just as I seldom saw her, I seldom thought of her either, until one day I was going home from school with my classmates through the convent park to the gate that led into the street when we heard a queer squawk. The chimney-sweep had just cleaned out the chimneys, having assured the nuns that the nesting time was past and the fledglings had all found their wings and flown away. Having swept the chimneys he had emptied his bag of soot on the compost heap in a corner of the park, which was made up for the most part of fallen leaves raked up by the old lay sister who took care of the garden. It was from this heap the squawk had come. Sitting up in the middle of the soot was a young jackdaw, fully grown but unfeathered, especially on the head and wings. A white down, of a sort, streaked with damp, only partially covered the rest of it, and its pink skin was everywhere shockingly exposed. At sight of us it gave another squawk, a squawk of fear.

Crying bitterly, we ran back to call the nuns, who came running out as helpless as ourselves. One of the young novices attempted to crawl towards the poor wretched creature thinking perhaps it could be put in a box in a warm place with a piece of flannel under it until it got stronger and could fly. But in its frantic struggle to get away from her, it sunk deeper into its morass. We were all crying when an old nun came out and told us there would be no chance at all of the mother bird coming back for it, if we touched it. Hadn't we been told never to foul a nest, never to handle the eggs, never to interfere with young birds? She despatched the novices back to the recreation room and comforting us as best she could led us out the gate.

During the night it rained and it's not likely any of us

slept much. Next day the bird was gone. No one knew what had happened to it. I'm sure the others soon forgot it. I never did. The poor bird reminded me of Alice who never wore a bow again in her hair, which got thinner and thinner.

Alice lived to be eighty years old. After she died, the old place was sold. When I heard the buildings were to be torn down I thought I'd drive down with two of my daughters to take a last look around. We didn't linger long in the empty house. It was bleak and desolate, and could not have been much different when Alice was alive. The girls shivered in the cold rooms. One of them made an effort to cheer me up by saying it was probable that lots of other houses in the old town would be just as bad if they were opened up to public view.

Another daughter came nearer the truth. 'Mother is not comparing it with anything in the present day. Isn't that right, Mother?' Delving into the pocket of her coat, 'Look what I found in a book I was reading before we left. I thought I'd bring it along for fun,' she said, producing the photograph of the old upstairs drawing-room. Creased, its glaze cracked, it still displayed unfaded indications of the former glories of the room. Seeing my mother's face, she faltered, 'I suppose it's not so funny to you, I shouldn't have shown it to you.'

Why not? I had let my children play with those old photos as I myself had, but without setting the same value on them as my mother had done. Few of them had survived. 'It must be hard for you to believe they are all dead?' my gentle daughter said.

'On the contrary, it's hard to believe they ever lived,' I said more lightheartedly than I felt. We were about to go downstairs when through a grimy window on the landing I caught sight of the loft to which as a child I had not gained access. The ladder with the top steps missing now had no steps at the bottom either. It hung by a remnant of its decayed handrail, and the weather-beaten door at the top had fallen inwards, all its hinges now gone. But to my amazement I saw that the old pieces of furniture I had dreamed of restoring to their former pride were still there. I even thought I caught a glint of gold leaf.

'Girls! Let's explore the old loft,' I cried. And, as molehills can be mountains to a child, mountains can be molehills to adults; we soon found a means of getting up there. It was hard for all three of us to find a place to stand with the mass of junk that went from floorboards to rafters, most of it as far as we could make out splintered or broken.

'It's a wonder this wasn't used for firewood,' Gloria said, picking up fragments of wood that were hand-carved and some of them exquisite examples of satinwood inlay. 'Do you think we could put some of those pieces together and take something home as a souvenir?'

'Why not try?' We set to work with a will and as energetically as possible in the cramped space, we found enough matching bits to put together a respectable number of beautiful odds and ends. We could have put together much more if we had had time at our disposal and room in the boot of our car. As it was, we retrieved a teapoy, a console, a lady's escritoire with delicately turned legs, and to the delight of the girls, intact, undamaged, a small admiralty chest with a secret drawer. Above all I had the joy of finding enough legs and rungs to put together two of those fragile, gilded Italian chairs, now so familiar to us in common metal reproductions. Stowing our loot into the car, the girls squabbled over the spoils of battle. Both were married but they had to have regard for their youngest sister recently engaged.

'What about you, Mother? Don't you want something? One of those little gold chairs? They are so pretty. One day they'll be priceless if they are not so already.' I shook my head. I didn't want anything.

My heart was no longer pierced by the past, but by the future. When those frail gold chairs were given new life, they, in all likelihood, would survive my beautiful daughters, as surely as they had survived the bevy of aunts.

A House to Let

'Over there, Bart, on the other side of the street,' Ella said, pointing to a vacant house, its uncurtained windows pasted with placards.

It was an evening in early spring and they were strolling back along Rathmines Road in the last of the light, going towards Ella's house, which was just off the main road. Ella's mother liked them to be home before eleven at latest, and she often had hot scones for them because Bart loved them, specially when they were hot with the butter melting on them and dripping through his fingers.

That winter the young couple had come to an understanding that they would marry, and they had told Ella's mother, but it wasn't a formal engagement although Bart had surprised Ella one evening recently by producing a little diamond ring from a beautiful purple-velvet casket that popped open when you pressed on a little pearl stud. Ella had been very worried at the expense of it, but Bart felt that it was worth it for the pleasure it would give her mother. He and her mother got on very well. And indeed it was her mother who suggested that Ella wouldn't wear the ring in public yet awhile, Ella only wore it when she went out alone with Bart in the evenings.

The ring was on Ella's finger that evening, as she pointed out the vacant house, although its lights were quenched in her little kid glove. If you looked closely you could see there was something lumpy about the third finger of her left hand. But who in the world ever looked that closely at anything? Ella herself couldn't see why some people, like the girls in the office, were so curious about other people's business. As far as she was concerned, her understanding with Bart hadn't made any difference at all, except that, now instead of going to the pictures of an evening, they'd taken to walking around the neighbouring streets looking vaguely at houses, just from the outside, of course.

Sometimes it seemed to Ella that Bart's interest in houses was the only difference their understanding had made in their relationship, although her mother seemed to think it had other important implications.

That spring there seemed to be a lot of houses for sale in Dublin, but the young couple seldom saw one to let and that was why Ella had pointed out the house although it was not a particularly nice house.

They looked across at it: it was a tall house with narrow windows and the hall-door was as narrow as the lid of a coffin. All the same they crossed the street to take a look.

'It says the key is next door,' Ella remarked, getting this information from a small hand-written note at the bottom of one of the auctioneer's notices. Usually the key had to be obtained from the auctioneer's office, and they weren't prepared to go to that length at this stage.

Ella looked the house over. The knocker had been painted black to save someone from having to shine it every day, and the garden in front was railed off so you couldn't get into it except from the basement of the house, and although a few dusty bushes of veronica had managed to flourish the garden was mainly ornamented by empty cigarette cartons, and toffee papers that had blown in from the street. Bart looked it over too, but with a man's practicality and calculation. 'I wouldn't take it as a present,' he said.

'Do you think I would,' Ella cried. 'I just thought it might be fun to go inside when the key is so handy.'

She hadn't known about the key until they'd crossed over, but she was slightly huffed by Bart's superior tone, but she hoped he hadn't noticed her small duplicity.

He hadn't. He was in fact looking at her the way he did when other fellows, lounging outside the pubs, or leaning over the parapet of the canal bridge whistled after them and he felt their whistling was a tribute to him as well as to her. 'I wonder what it is like inside,' he said suddenly.

Ella wasn't interested but it did cross her mind that it would be nice for once in a way to get in out of the streets, and be together wandering around the empty rooms of the old house. But whatever store her mother put on their understanding Ella felt pretty sure it wouldn't allow for breaking the proprieties.

'Perhaps – ' she began.

But Bart didn't wait to hear. 'I'll get the key,' he cried, breaking away from her.

Surprised by his abrupt change of mind. Ella stood and watched him as he ran up the steps of the neighbouring house, taking them two at a time, and knocked, too loud Ella thought, on the door. A minute later the door was opened by a thin woman in black, a landlady no doubt, because even at that distance Ella could see the curiosity in her eyes. Then the woman vanished into the narrow hallway, and when she reappeared she handed Bart a key with a big label on it like a luggage label.

'I have it!' Bart said and when he reached her he caught her arm almost roughly. 'Come on, let's go inside.'

Ella stared. Why was he so excited? A few minutes earlier he hadn't wanted to see the house at all. Now he was practically dragging her after him up the steps in his eagerness and haste.

On the top step Ella withdrew her arm. 'I'm sorry we bothered,' she said. 'It's getting late. Mother will be expecting us. And it's getting dark too; we won't be able to see it properly. She seemed to have forgotten that it was she who had suggested looking at it in the first place. Now she was looking critically at it, and, for that matter, at Bart too. 'What good will it do us to see it? It's too big for us, and the rent will be too much, and anyway it's ugly, really ugly. She had a moment of compunction when she saw Bart stare confused at the key in his hand. 'I suppose we'll have to make some use of the key, since we gave that woman the trouble of getting it for us,' she said and she glanced vindictively at the windows of the other house. 'She's probably staring out at us this minute from behind her hideous curtains.'

Bart looked again at the other house. He could see no one, but not for a moment did he doubt that Ella might possess superior vision. And as he was looking, it crossed his mind, humbly, that in the matter of curtains too, if he was not guided by Ella's good taste, he himself would not have thought them too bad. And for the hundredth time since he'd persuaded her to join her lot with his, he acknowledged silently to himself that without her he would at best have blundered through life, never knowing by what a hair's breadth good taste differed from its counterfeit. 'Well, what will we do? Will we just take a quick look'? he asked.

'Oh, it's not worth the bother.' Ella said.

Her tone stung him. 'It was your idea, Ella.'

Ella couldn't deny that. 'How quick you were to take me up on it. All the same!' she said.

They stared at each other. Then Bart turned, shoved the key in the lock, and went to turn it, at the same time putting his shoulder to the door, and pushing it.

'Do you want to break the lock?' Ella asked coldly. 'Here, let me try,' she said, and she took off her gloves. Then after one deft twist of her slender wrist the key turned easily and the door opened. 'Ugh!' she said. 'Such a smell,' drawing back from the breath of foul air that came out from the dark hall-way. It was probably only a smell of damp, but it had a sickly sweetness too, a sort of mushroomy smell, as if, unseen, the timbers had begun to rot and sprout with some disgusting fungus. She shuddered.

Yet Bart's eagerness had increased. 'Come on, Ella,' he cried and not waiting for her to pass ahead of him, he stepped into the hall. The darkness, the odours, he did not notice at all. He was suddenly as excited as if they were about to enter into some mysterious cavern where ecstasy and rapture awaited them. For an instant, before flinging himself headlong into the hallway he turned and laced Ella to him, and as if the transports that awaited them might be too much for her he felt like reaching out and laying his hand over her eyes to protect her.

To his astonishment Ella pushed him away and stepped back.

'I'll wait outside here, Bart,' she said. 'You go in, and take a look around and tell me what it's like.'

Bart stared at her. 'Do you mean to tell me you're not coming in?' He couldn't believe he had heard her rightly. What was wrong? Disappointment made him dumb.

'I might go in, if there's time when you come out,' she

said after a minute. 'But be quick, will you, Bart; the light is
fading.'

'Why won't you come in with me?' he demanded. An
awful thought had struck him. Did she not trust him? Was
that it? Did she think – ?

Ella, however, had taken out the small enamel powder-
box he'd given her a year before, and opening it she was
peering into the mirrored lid, absorbed in her own image.
'It's better for us to go in one at a time,' she said. 'You hear
such queer things about empty houses. If anything
happened to you, or there was anyone hiding in there, you
could call out and I could run for help.'

Bart burst out laughing with relief and amusement.
Perhaps I won't bother going in at all,' he said, because
now he too saw that it was very dank and unpleasant and
indeed Ella was right about it being dank and evil-
smelling. Just the same, curiosity forced him in a few paces,
and seeing a door on the right, he opened it and went into a
large empty room, dimly lit by a north window. 'There's a
fine mantelpiece in here,' he called out to Ella.

'I thought there might be,' she called back, 'because that
amber door-knob is so beautiful.'

'What door-knob?' He looked back at it. Those old
fashioned glass knobs had never appealed to him, and in
any case he couldn't see what it had to do with the
mantelpiece. The mantelpiece was like one you'd see in an
auction-room on the quays. 'You ought to see it, Ella,' he
called out.

'You can tell me about it later,' Ella called in. 'I wish
you'd hurry, Bart. It's getting dark.'

Bart came back into the hall and closed the door. He
looked up the steep stairs. Would he bother going up? 'I'll
just take one quick look upstairs,' he said.

Ella saw his long legs disappearing up the uncarpeted stairs. Why on earth had she pointed out the wretched house to him? She was not only impatient, she was beginning to feel cold standing there on the chilly steps. And as the minutes went by she grew irritable. 'Are you all right, Bart?' she called up, although she could hear his feet travelling over the floor-boards overhead. He seemed determined to go into every single room. She got more and more irritable. So like a man, she thought, tiresome and without thought for others. 'Bart. For heaven's sake!' she called out, but what with opening and shutting doors, and banging shutters he probably didn't hear her. How well he had never suggested going into one of those nice little red-brick terraced houses off Appian Way that he knew she admired, one with a bay window to one side of the door, and a nice little garden that nobody would throw papers into because the road was like a private road. But oh no, Bart never suggested going in and looking around one of those little houses. Trust a man, even a man like Bart she conceded, to be cautious when it came anywhere near taking the final step.

Ella drew her collar closer to her neck and shivered. Spring or no spring there was a sting in the air. She forgot completely about the small diamond whose lights were, once more, quenched under her glove. She was so indignant with him she didn't hear him coming down the stairs, and didn't realize he was standing beside her until he slammed the hall door.

'Oh Bart, you startled me,' she said crossly, but as he took the key out of the lock she felt obliged to ask what the upstairs rooms were like.

'I'll tell you later,' Bart said. 'I want to get rid of this key.'

When he came back he put his arm around her waist.

'Please, Bart!' she protested, and although it was really dark now she tried to free herself from his encircling arm. She was warm and comfortable with his arm around her but they weren't the only people in the street. 'Be careful!' she warned him. 'What would people think?'

'Let them think what they like,' he said, and he tightened his arm around her waist. 'We needn't worry about what people might think of us in a locality like this.' There was a new and derogatory note in his voice. Then, as if he had read the thoughts that passed through her mind while she was waiting on the steps for him, he said something that brought a lump to her throat and made her want to cry. 'It would be a different matter altogether if this was one of the little roads off Appian Way, the ones you like, with those nice little red-brick houses. We wouldn't want to give the people there a bad opinion of us.'

Ella partly guessed what was in his mind, but she managed to ask what he meant in a small, low voice. 'Why?' she asked.

Because that's the kind of road we're going to live on, isn't it?' he asked. His voice rose. 'How is it that we never see one of those little houses vacant? I'll tell you why. It's because they are in such demand. That's why. They are no sooner vacant than they are snapped up again. And I'll tell you something else, Ella. We ought to keep our eyes open: we ought to be more on the alert. It's all very well to say that we're not getting married immediately, but there are things that ought to be taken into consideration, like the housing situation. How do we know that there will be a suitable house available when we finally make up our minds about a date?'

They had started to walk along the street again but Bart stopped suddenly and wheeled her around to face him.

'I'm telling you, Ella, it's not a bit too soon to start house hunting in earnest. As a matter of fact we should have begun long ago. We've lost a lot of valuable time already.' Then he squared his shoulders. 'That can't be helped now, of course, but from tonight on I've made up my mind that if we do come across a suitable house I'm not going to let it slip. Do you hear me, Ella?'

Yes, Ella had heard him, but she didn't answer. Under the pale light of a street lamp, she was afraid he might see her face and she turned aside so he wouldn't know she was laughing.

He had seen though. 'You're laughing,' he said accusingly. Yes she was. Her whole body was trembling with laughter.

'I'd like to know what you find so funny.'

But Ella herself didn't know why she was laughing. It was just that a lot of things seemed suddenly to have come together but with such a right result. Looking at the house had seemed so purposeless, such a waste of time, and yet, in the course of the few minutes he had spent inside and she had waited on the steps, some incalculable force had worked upon him, and their destiny together had been advanced to a point from which now they would race forward.

How strange it all was. How little part one seemed to play in determining the course of one's life.

She looked at him. Above all, how different a man was from a woman. So different, she thought, as she pressed closer to him going along the street and suddenly she felt a passionate longing for the time when they would explore those differences to the full.